LAST NOTE

By

Gill Burnett

Copyright © Gill Burnett 2024
This book is sold subject to the condition that it shall not, by way of trade or otherwise, be lent, resold, hired out, or otherwise circulated without the publisher's prior consent in any form of binding or cover other than that in which it is published and without a similar condition including this condition being imposed on the subsequent publisher.
The moral right of Gill Burnett has been asserted.
ISBN: 9798327032859

This is a work of fiction. Names, characters, businesses, organisations, places, events and incidents either are the product of the author's imagination or are used fictitiously. Any resemblance to actual persons, living or dead, events, or locales is entirely coincidental.

For Joan, my Mam,
for always reading every word I write x

"Let us not be satisfied with just giving money. Money is not enough, money can be got, but they need your hearts to love them. So, spread your love everywhere you go."

Mother Teresa

CONTENTS

Prologue *1*
1 You Can't Take It With You! *3*
2 The Penny Drops *5*
3 A Bad Penny *18*
4 Penny Dreadful *36*
5 Hand to Mouth *46*
6 Look After the Pennies and the Pounds Will Look After Themselves *59*
7 Worth Your Weight in Gold *67*
8 Money for Nothing *79*
9 A Pretty Penny *91*
10 Fool's Gold *102*
11 In for a Penny in for a Pound *126*
12 The Best That Money Can Buy! *142*
13 Gold Digger *163*
14 Take the Money and Run *187*
15 Creative Accounting *203*
16 They Know the Cost of Everything and the Value of Nothing! .. *219*
17 Show Me the Money!! *233*
18 Cross My Palm *248*
19 Money for Old Rope *260*
20 More Money Than Sense! *272*
21 Love of Money is the Root of All Evil *289*
22 Whip Round! *300*
Epilogue *312*

Prologue

What is a £10 note worth now to what it was ten years ago?? Not as much, but still to me it is priceless. Especially £10 note HE75229564 .

The Covid 19 Pandemic has almost rendered us a cashless society. It is all contact this and contact that these days.

And even though we all know there will always be currency in some form, with the passing of late Queen Elizabeth II and the ascension of King Charles III, the good old fashioned £10 note will be a thing of the past.

But for those of you that know me and have read my 'Notes' books, you will know that I first began following £10 note HE75229564 back in 2012. Ten years ago!!!

In 2016/17 I went back to revisit all of the people who had HE75229564 in their possession along with a few people who were red herrings when we thought the note had gone one way when in actual fact it had gone another. We all have a story to tell!

I like to think that I have built up relationships with all of my 'Noters' as I like to call them. Some I would actually deem as friends. In the intervening years I have continued to stay in touch with virtually all of them.

It was some of their suggestions that I go back and

see them one last time. Ten years is a long time. Ten years can give us so much more than a snapshot on their lives.

So that is what I have done. I have gone back and found each and every one of them. By hook and by crook because some of them aren't where I left them. And I have laughed and I have cried with them.

It has been the most amazing experience of my life getting to know all of these people.

It started with my good friend and neighbour Rita Simmonds. And once again that is where we will begin.

But our beginning was her end. I still miss her and I truly would not be the writer I am today without her. So Rita, if you are looking down on me; thank you from the bottom of my heart!

1

You Can't Take It With You!

Rita Simmonds died just as my second book was going to print. She had been 84 years old and according to her daughter Christine, she had just not felt herself as she took herself off to bed. When Christine had gone to check on her an hour or so later, she was gone.

It had been peaceful, just like Rita Simmonds had deserved. Rita Simmonds and her fastidious keeper of bank note serial numbers literally changed my life. It was Rita that planted the seed for writing my dissertation, that resulted in me publishing my first book, Take Note and the subsequent Note Taken and although at that point I had no ambition to write a third about £10 note HE75229564, here I am.

Of course I attended her funeral, as did my mam, we had been neighbours for many years before she moved into her daughter Christine's garage come Granny flat and she had been my friend. I had often popped to see her over the years. She was my biggest fan.

And as funerals go it was lovely. It was a celebration with her daughter Christine now well on her way to becoming a cleric, she did not take the funeral herself, it had been the parish Vicar, Rev Stephens who did that. But Christine did a reading and read the eulogy.

It was a lovely eulogy, full of love. And of course, it was bittersweet. Christine talked about her mam being reunited with not just Rita's own husband, but Christine's too and her two sons who had all so tragically died in a car crash.

I only stayed for the service. They would all be returning to Christine's afterwards, but I did not want to intrude.

Rita Simmonds Nee Cushing

11/10/1934 – 28/02/2018

Always remembered.

2

The Penny Drops

Kate Lockey was Rita Simmons' granddaughter. Kate was a recipient of £10 note HE75229564. It had been given to her by Rita Simmonds as part of her 21st birthday present.

But Kate hadn't kept it for long. It was in one hand and out the other within hours. Passed over to the useless piece of work who she called her boyfriend. Adam Mitchell.

The £10 note HE75229564 had been both Adam Mitchell's downfall and redemption.

The Adam Mitchell of back then was very different to the Adam Mitchell of today. Back then he was a petty thief, a cheat, a liar. Kate Lockey had been infatuated with him; blind to him and his ways. He had Kate wrapped around his little finger; he was her life.

But that was before everything happened.

That was before Kate watched Adam Mitchell get sent to prison.

It had been the making of both of them. Kate Lockey became savvy. Adam grew up and even though Kate had no intention of ever seeing Adam again once he had been sent down, she found herself making the journey to the Wakefield prison that housed him and fell in love with Adam all over again.

But this time he was different. What had happened to him had made him grow up, the new version was more focused; less jumpy. There was nothing to be looking over his shoulder for. He was in prison, there were no dodgy dealing to be done or if there was he wasn't getting himself involved and there were no girls.

Kate adored him. Though she wasn't so green that she didn't have the thought in the back of her head that he would resort to form once he was out and about in the wide world again. So Kate kept Adam a secret and continued to visit, all the while keeping up the façade that she was young free and single and simply enjoying her life without Adam Mitchell.

But on release day it was Kate collecting Adam from outside the prison. It was Kate who had booked a swanky hotel so they could have some luxury and above all else privacy on his first night of freedom and it was Kate who made sure that Adam had a new collection of clothes to wear once the stench of prison was washed off him. This again was something that Kate did for him. She soaped his body to within an inch of its life. It was the best night of both Kate and Adam's life.

But Kate continued to keep Adam a secret. She didn't want to jinx it; she didn't want to be left with egg on her face when if or more than likely when Adam was caught with some other girl. But he hadn't seemed to. Adam embraced his freedom, embraced the fact that he had somehow managed to have Kate back into his life. He really seemed to have changed. He got a steady job and had a regular income, no need to beg, steal or borrow off Kate anymore. Yet still she kept the fact that her and Adam were an item again tightly under wraps. It ate at her but she needed to be sure and as the weeks passed and her confidence grew in the relationship she knew that she needed to tell her mam and dad.

They were nice people. They only had Kate's interests at heart and she knew that once they saw the change in Adam, they would have no reason to worry. The Adam Mitchell who her mam and dad had last seen in a court room waiting to be sent to prison was long gone. He was cleaner now, in all ways and Kate could only hope that everyone would forgive him his past discretions and see how happy they were.

But Kate didn't get chance to tell them.

There was that fateful night that changed everything forever. The night that Kate's dad and brothers had been involved in a fatal car accident and had gone forever. The guilt about not telling them ate at Kate as much as the grief did.

For the months and months that followed Kate and her mam lived in some type of black cloud, nothing got through to them. Not even Adam. All thoughts of him had been out to one side and for that time it was just Kate and Christine shrouded in grief. They went nowhere apart to her Nana's once a week, even that was an ordeal that neither of them ever wanted to make. But they did it, they had each other, not that they interacted much, but Rita Simmons was on her own. So a weekly pilgrimage to see her was really not too much to ask.

Kate quit her job. She would never go back there, that had been part of her life before the accident. When she was ready, she would look for something else. Until then they would just sit. Though neither Christine or Kate had any idea what it was they were waiting for, they would never feel normal again so what exactly could it be that they were waiting for.

And then there was Reverend Stephens.

He had called one day to see Christine and that was the beginning of the cocoon of grief and hopelessness beginning to lift. It was by no means a miracle or anything. It just felt like after his first visit, Christine didn't seem so bereft.

Kate had no belief in God. How could there be a God who would allow her Dad, Liam and Niall to die like that. But for some reason, Christine seemed to have found some faith and Kate was shocked when on the next Sunday morning Christine was up and dressed smartly and off to Church.

And then there was Adam.

Maybe that was some sort of a miracle. It had been Christine's idea to find him and get him over to see Kate. With the help of Reverend Stephens that was what had happened and at the very sight of him Kate could feel a small drop of ice fall off her frozen heart.

From then on in it was Kate and Adam. Christine not only allowed Adam into their house, but into their lives. It was a slow process but it made progress and the three of them settled into some sort of existence.

Christine found her faith, big style. She took comfort from it, loved the tradition of it and in what was a shock to Kate, began her ministry to become a priest, all with the help who turned out to be an extremely good friend, Reverend Stephens.

Kate went to college, unsure at first about what the end outcome would be when she finished the access into healthcare course but always with an eye on maybe securing a place at university to train to become a paramedic. In Kate's mind it was a way of giving something back to society. The world had been robbed of her dad, Liam and Niall and whatever contribution they made, it was just something she wanted to do.

And she did.

Now Kate Lockey is Kate Mitchell.

The intervening years had not been easy. University had been a lot harder than she could ever have thought they would be, especially when she began training with an ambulance crew. The first road traffic accident she had attended had made her be actually sick. But she had dug deep and overcame it. She was there to help, something that her lost family had never had the opportunity to be given. By the time the emergency services got to the accident all five people in the two cars were dead.

At home the house once again became a home. It had been a mausoleum for so long, the sadness around the place was almost tangible. But Christine had managed to persuade Kate's nan, Rita Simmons to give up her home and move in with them. It had been a long and laborious task. Her nan had lived in her little house all her married life. It was her sanctuary and had always thought that she would have ended her days there. But Christine had been persistent, encouraged; cajoled and in the end simply told her that Christine and Kate needed her. Enough said. The packing began.

And at their house, the ordeal of emptying the garage so that the builders could begin the conversion was put off and put off until the end it was like the Elastoplast effect and Kate, Christine and Adam emptied the garage the weekend before the builders were due to begin.

It was very much Mark, Kate's dad's man cave. It even had the smell of him. Mementos of Kate's childhood were everywhere. The boys' bikes, skateboards, boxing gloves. There were so many things belonging to the men who no longer lived in the house. When the house had been cleared about 6 months after they died, it had taken Christine and Kate weeks. It had been such a harrowing thing to do. What to be thrown out, what to keep, what to donate to charity. Every day Reverend Stephens came and collected the piles and piles of black bin bags to take to a local charity. Even with a bit more distance between their death and the garage clearance, it was as hard as ever.

The garage was a condensed space full of all three of the mens belongings; aside from an old exercise bike and a couple of dolls houses belonging to Kate; it was all Mark, Liam and Niall. If it hadn't been for Adam being there and encouraging them; the garage would have been left as was, the builders cancelled and Rita Simmonds left in her little terrace house on the other side of town.

But like everything else they had to do, they got through it. The builders came and the man cave was slowly turned into a 'Granny flat' and by the time Adam had put the last lick of paint on the wall; it little resembled the garage as was.

Rita came to live there, Adam stayed in the beginning until it made more sense for him to move his meagre belonging into the house too. The house came alive again. Not as it was when it was a family of 5; mam, dad and children. This time it had a different type of tempo. There were good days and bad days, but what had been the constant feel of sadness; now there seemed to be peace.

Christine took to her calling with relish. It was a calling. She was never happier than when she was helping others. She had so much empathy with people; especially the bereaved. She went on retreats and attended courses all around the country. Somewhere along the way she decided that she did not want to become a priest; she would like to be a curate. It would give her more time to spend with parishioners; there would not be the pull on her time to attend meetings with the Bishop and such like. Reverend Stephens was encouraging and when his wife left him and the vicarage, it was Christine that got him through his darkest days. Just like he had her.

Kate often wondered if there was more than to the relationship between her mam and the Reverend, but she never asked. They were close. But Kate knew in her heart of hearts that even though Reverend Stephens seemed her mam's plus one on many occasions; her heart belonged to her dad. But it made Kate worry about her mam less knowing that she had someone in her life that she could rely on.

Adam had proposed and Kate accepted. There was no reason not to. They had decided on just a small wedding, obviously it would be Reverend Stephens who would marry them, even though Kate still wasn't convinced about the whole God thing; her mam was and to somewhat so was Adam.

Reverend Stephens, Rita and Adam would often sit together and talk about God and the bible and their own faith. It was something that always made Kate smile; where had the other Adam Mitchell got to?

So a date for the wedding was set, immediate family only followed by a few drinks at the house and then Kate and Adam would go away for a week's honeymoon, if Adam could get a passport in time. But then as things tend to do, it all went a bit tits up when Rita died.

Kate took her nan's passing badly. Not so much that Rita had died, she was a good age and although she was in good health, she was old and had all the complications that came with that. It was more the process of her passing, the condolences the funeral, the empty 'Granny flat'. The shifting of the tempo of the house again.

And then there was Adam. For some reason Adam and Rita had struck up a lovely relationship. They would often play cards on a winter's night together or if the weather was good, they would sit in the garden chatting drinking milky coffee or sometimes having a bottle of beer, or in her nan's case a shandy. He was so upset when she died. But Kate couldn't handle it or him and pushed him away.

The wedding was cancelled out of respect and the memento of getting it rebooked seemed to be lost to both of them. Even after Adam's passport arrived on the day of Rita's funeral, something that Adam said was a gift from her Nan, they still couldn't summon up enough mojo to do anything about getting the ball rolling again.

Kate and Adam drifted apart. Even though Adam officially lived with Kate at her mam's house, she actively encouraged him to stay at his mam's house when he was working late, which he often did. He was self-employed and time was money.

So, for months and months they became distant from one another. They went through the motions of being a couple but there was nothing there. Kate was a cold fish, she knew she was, if Adam came anywhere near her, she would physically freeze. He kept trying, not for sex, just for affection, but he got nothing.

Adam was grieving just as she was, he just didn't have the open scars that Kate did after the loss of her dad and her brothers. She couldn't help him.

It wasn't until he started to stay at his mam's more

and more did something wake up inside her. Adam was the love of her life, her only love. When she thought about it he hadn't tried to get close to her for weeks. All at once everything clicked into place. She was being a fool. She didn't want to live the rest of her life without Adam too, she had lost enough already.

She reached out. First just texts and the odd phone call. She was trying to build bridges. But he was distant; alarm bells started to ring. Adam sounded like old Adam. The Adam that used to cheat on her time after time. Had he met someone else? Had she pushed him away so hard he had fell in to the comforting arms of someone else?

But she wouldn't give up, not without a fight. Kate at least needed to try and salvage their relationship. So, the texts and phone calls then became a night at the pictures or a meal. The feeling that he had met someone else was still there, he didn't say, and she didn't ask. She didn't want to know. It was all her fault if he had. All she could do was keep at it, the contact, the dates and by the time that Rita's first year of passing was upon them, Covid 19 had arrived along with the lockdown and restrictions and Kate and Adam were a couple again.

The thought of going through the whole lockdown without Adam was scary. She had been so close to blowing it all. Kate worked through it, she had little choice, Adam worked through it too, the amount of businesses taking the opportunity to have their offices and workspaces decorated whilst they were empty was mind blowing. But still; nearly everything was closed and it would have been totally soul-destroying spending day after day and night after night on her own.

This time the wedding was arranged, the honeymoon booked and on Christmas Eve, Kate Lockey became Mrs Adam Mitchell in a small ceremony at Christine's Church. It was perfect. Well as perfect as it could be with so many people missing. 'Just because we can't see them, it doesn't mean that they not here!' Christine's words before she walked her daughter, her only surviving child down the aisle nearly made Kate lose it. Her faith may not have been as strong as her mam's was, but she liked to think what she said to Kate was true and that her Dad, her brothers and her nan were all there watching her make her vows to the man she loved.

And how she loved Adam.

Married life suited them. They still lived at Christine's house where they were mainly left to their own devices, Christine was always so busy now she was a curate and for some reason only known to Christine, she tended to stay in the 'Granny Flat' most of the time. Kate wasn't sure if it was to give her and Adam their privacy or that the bedroom that she had shared for so long with Mark was holding her back. Reverend Stephens was still very much her plus one, but it was only a subject that she would speculate with Adam with and never talk to her mam about.

Kate was a fully-fledged paramedic; she loved it. If Christine had found her vocation, then so had Kate. Like her mam, she had empathy with her patients and their families. She could not imagine doing anything else for a job.

Adam's business continues to grow, he had even taken another lad on to help him. There was little of Adam Mitchell of 10 years earlier, Kate could not have been prouder.

Kate Mitchell nee Lockey was now 31 years old. A woman. People asked her all the time when her and Adam would be starting a family. It was something they had talked about a lot. And they decided that they didn't want children. It shocked people, even if they didn't say anything, Kate could see it in their faces. Kate had worked with children when she was younger, she liked children. It was just something that wasn't for her and Adam. It may have been the fear factor on Kate's part, a child would be something else that she could lose, but she wasn't sure. Maybe later, as her biological clocked ticked away she may feel different. But that would be a decision that Kate and Adam would make together.

Kate and Adam together! No one would have given them a hope in hell when Kate was 21. When the penny dropped; she hadn't herself. But time and circumstances had changed everything in a good and a bad way. Kate Mitchell was happy, or as happy as anyone could be who had been through the tragedy that she had. But time heals and hope prevails……

'How lucky I am to have something that makes saying goodbye so hard.'
Winnie the Pooh

3

A Bad Penny

Adam Mitchell received £10 note HE75229564 amongst the £50 that his girlfriend Kate Lockey had lent to him on the night of her 21st birthday. The night that Adam had put the £50 on a greyhound that was a dead cert and hadn't even made it around the first bend and the same night that Adam was arrested and subsequently sent to prison.

Now at 35, Adam Mitchell still has kept his boyish good looks. The hairline is receding a bit, but the twinkly blue eyes and the toned physique remain. Ten years earlier his pallor was always grey thanks to his terrible lifestyle. Now he looked a picture of health.

The reputation that his name carried now was more for his painting and decorating skills and less and not so much for his drinking, drugs, women and criminal activities. Not that people had forgotten. He still bumped into people who liked to regale him with stories of Adam Mitchell of old.

Adam could expect no less. He had been to prison for God's Sake, people wouldn't forget that. But if someone mentioned the fact that he had been incarcerated, then Adam would simply say that being sent down had been the making of him. He had served his time, learned a big lesson and never looked back.

If people worried about letting a convicted petty criminal into their homes, it didn't affect his business. Adam liked to think that he had a name for doing a good job, at a fair price and customers knew that if he thought that something wasn't going to work, he would advise against and suggest an alternative. His waiting list was ever growing.

For Adam that felt good.

In his mam's eyes he was back to the young teenage boy who used to be her pride and joy. 'Your granddad would be so proud of you' was like music to his ears when she would chirp it to him. It just felt so much nicer to be nice.

And then there was Kate. He had no idea how he had got her back in his life. When he was sent to prison, he thought that had been that. The look on her face when he had been led out of the courtroom had broken his heart. He deserved nothing less than the prison sentence and the broken heart. But away from all the trappings and temptation of the outside world, he knew that he had to at least try to not only turn his life around but win back Kate's heart.

It had been slowly, slowly catches the worm. Kate came to the prison to see him. It was a reset moment and from then on in, with the communication lines open, he did everything he could to prove to Kate that he was not only a changed man, but someone she could spend the rest of her life with.

They kept everything low key, under the radar so to speak, Kate didn't want people to know until they were certain, or more so, Kate could trust him. So on his release he took on a warehouse job, thanks to the forklift truck course he had taken years earlier thanks to the Jobcentre sending him on a course and the intervention of his probation officer. And he continued to keep his nose clean.

It wasn't a walk in the park by any means. The majority of his friends were the friends that he had worked with before prison and who were still doing what they were doing when he left them. Adam being sent to prison didn't seem to put them off, but Adam knew himself that once you had that lifestyle there was limited chance to get out unless you took Adam's route or worse.

So, Adam worked and saw Kate and did little else in between, which was fine. He was happy with his lot. Kate had decided that she was going to tell her family and friends that they were an item again, better she did than someone else, it was a small town and people talked. Guilt wasn't something that suited Kate, unlike Adam who had done so much that should have made him feel guilty it only took something mammoth like going to prison that set his nerves on end.

And then Kate was gone. The tragedy of the car crash killing her dad and brothers sent her into a place she could only be on her own. There was no room for Adam. All he could do was wait, wait for her to reach out. He thought that maybe happen after the funeral, but seeing her there she looked like a fragile flower that would crumble at any time. Adam knew that Kate would not be back with him any time soon, if ever.

It broke Adam's heart. But his heart would be nowhere near as broken as Kate or her mam's. His own life would have to go on without her. It would have been so easy to revert to his old ways, head for the pub. Drink, drugs, women. It was a massive temptation, the thought of losing himself even for a few hours was literally a five-minute walk from his mam's house. But Adam knew it wouldn't just be one night. He knew that if he went on a bender, he would do it again and again and before he knew it he would have lost his job at the warehouse, which to be fair wasn't the job of his dreams, but paid a good wage and gave him some timetable to his life.

Then what if Kate did get in touch and he had reverted back to Adam of old. What use would he be to her?? And if she didn't come back then at least he had to have some sort of meaning to his life without her, one that didn't involve bed hopping and driving stolen cars. But still, the thought of having a laugh in the pubs with his mates weighed heavy on him.

And then as if by magic he spotted an advert for a painting and decorating course. It was something he had always liked, when he was younger, he liked nothing better than helping his mam make their shabby living room into something pristine. The course was expensive, but he could afford it, better on a course than in a pub's till. So he enrolled, booked two weeks off from his job at the warehouse and added a new layer to the onion that was Adam Mitchell.

Adam loved his course. He loved working with his hands. He found that working with his hands steadied his mind. The temptation of the pub and drugs and women waned and he spent his time practising his new found skills on his mam's house. She was over the moon!

Then came the telephone call off Reverend Stephens about going to see Kate. And the rest as they say is history, or it should have been. It took time, she was so fragile, but together they took it one day at a time, the three of them. Who would ever of thought that Kate's mam, Christine would welcome him into her home and lives with open arms. But she did and their home became Adam's second home and when it was suggested that he move in with them, he did.

And then Kate's nan Rita came too. Adam was given the task of decorating the recently refurbished garage where Rita would live. It had been a privilege, Rita had given him an idea what she would like, Adam had worked his magic. It was the beginning of an unexpected friendship between Adam and Rita. Adam cherished her, always made time for her and could often be found sitting in the 'Granny Flat' playing a game of switch with Rita and sometimes Christine too.

Kate and Christine were still hurting, they would probably never be the same people they had been before the accident. But they all moseyed along together. Adam packed in his job at the warehouse with the support of Kate and Christine and struck out on his own using all his new found painting and decorating skills. He never looked back.

When Kate accepted his offer of marriage his life was complete.

Reverend Stephens agreed to marry them, Reverend Stephens who became a regular visitor at the house. Who was supporting Christine as her journey through her training and who also had struck up a friendship with Rita and became a regular player of cards in the 'Granny Flat' too. Adam liked him. He had never met a vicar before, but Reverend Stephens had a wicked sense of humour and had a way of making in the most difficult situations seems achievable.

If Adam was honest, even though the house was still tinged with sadness, it was the happiest time of Adam's life. He had Kate's love, a flourishing business, friendship in the form of Christine, Rita and the Rev as Adam called him. Adam was so far removed from old Adam it beggared belief. But then life has a way of kicking you in the teeth when you least expect it, it's like the universe says 'you're getting a little bit too big for your boots!' And sends in a hand grenade.

The hand grenade was Rita Simmons' death. Adam's friend, Kate's nan, Christine's mam. And before he knew it Kate's grief was all consuming again and he was back out in the cold. This time he was hurting too. When Kate had lost her dad and her brothers, Adam had been a step removed from it. Kate's younger brother Niall had been a school friend, but they weren't close. Or maybe they were, Niall had invited Adam to his 21st Birthday party; that's where he had met Kate, but Adam had no recollection of them even seeing much of each other since leaving school, they moved in very different circles.

This time is was different; he had made a friend of Rita. The house was so empty and so quiet without her, or maybe that was because both Kate and Christine had retreated back to the place they had been after the boys had gone. Adam didn't know what to do. He tried to talk to Kate but there was nothing, the shutters were down and no matter how many times he tried, she was lost to him again.

The only thing he could do was work hard, be there for them if they needed him, but as the funeral passed it was obvious that Kate didn't want him there so he packed up his belongings and went to stay at his mam's house.

Once again the temptation to go blow off some steam was eating away at him. Kate didn't want him. He met up with the Rev. As he sat in a Costa in town with the vicar, dog collar and all he wondered what his old friends would make of him. He really had come a long way. The Rev's advice was just to wait. All Kate and Christine's old wounds had been opened, they would have been grieving for Rita anyway, but what had gone before just made Rita's passing a million times worse. Wait and be patient was the Rev's advice. What else could he do.

So, he worked day and night. Filled up the emptiness with manual labour, worked so hard that when he climbed into his bed a night he slept soundly and there was little opportunity to fall off the wagon. But that wasn't strictly true. He might not have gone on the drink or took drugs or stole anything. But then there was Wendy!!!

Adam's job as a painter and decorator gave him contact with lots of females. Lots and lots of them. In the close proximately of their homes they would flirt for England with him. Ever the charmer, Adam would flirt back. But that was as far as it ever went. Most of them had husbands or partners who Adam had met when he had gone to do the original estimate. But still they flirted. Old Adam would have been all over them, husbands or not. But Adam had Kate and he didn't ever want to give her any reason not to trust him. So he flirted which usually resulted in biscuits with his tea and a hefty tip or crate of beer at the end of the job. Method in his madness. Flattered as he always was, the tea and biscuits was as far as it ever went.

That was before Rita died and Kate retreated.

The truth of the matter he was as lost as Kate was. Lost without Kate. She made him want to be a better person. He missed Rita, she had been a wise old owl, she knew a lot of stuff about a lot of stuff. And he missed living at the house. Being back in his old bedroom made him feel a bit of a failure; it was like a big step backwards. And worse than that, he was back where he started and he hadn't done anything wrong. He was new Adam now, Adam on the up, Adam who was running his own small business and keeping out of trouble.

He was trying his best to stay focused. Kate would

get in touch; he had been sure of it when he first arrived back at his mam's house. He hadn't even unpacked his bag. But as the days passed and the weeks went by he began to doubt whether she would. All he could do was work and wait.

It was the work that brought Wendy into his life. Wendy and her wonky wallpaper.

Adam had been recommended to Wendy by a friend she played golf with she told him over the phone when she called to see if he could give her an estimate. She named names; Adam remembered her, she had been a bit of a pain in the neck, fur coat and no knickers his mam would have called her. He remembered her well because he had to chase her for weeks to get paid off her. Despite the swanky house he had decorated, she seemed to be asset rich and cash poor. It wasn't something he would divulge to Wendy over the telephone so just said yes he remembered her vaguely.

Anyway Adam arranged to go to Wendy's house a few days later, which he did and was greeted by a very jolly lady who proceeded to tell him that she had lived in the house a few years and even though it was only rented accommodation, she couldn't live with the wallpaper in her living room any longer.

Adam could see why the minute she showed him into the room, the whole room seemed to be a little off kilter. There was a distinct pattern to the wallpaper, but who ever had put it up must have put the first strip on slightly skewwhiff and had unfortunately used that strip to set up the rest of the room. It made the whole room appear to be slightly wonky. At first glance you probably wouldn't be able to see it, but it was one of those things that once you had seen it you couldn't unsee it.

Wendy said it was driving her mad. A price to re-paper the walls and paint all the walls and ceilings was agreed and Wendy said she would call him once the original paper was removed and they could arrange a date.

And that was the last he heard from Wendy for a couple of weeks until he got a text message saying it was her and that the living room was now upright and he if he could come as soon as was humanly possible, she had shopped and had everything ready for him.

The text made him laugh, not something he had done much of up to that point. He knew what Wendy meant though, so checked his diary, fired off the date along with lots of smiley faces. Wendy messaged him back, along with a picture of one of the new rolls of wallpaper which had big circles and resembled nothing of the wallpaper recently unstuck from Wendy's wonky wall.

Whether it was because Adam was bored or he was lonely, but the messages continued to fly backwards and forwards. Wendy was very funny. Adam found himself looking forward to his mobile phone bleeping announcing the arrival of a message.

They messaged so much that by the time he arrived at Wendy's house with his paintbrush in hand, it was like meeting an old friend.

Wendy knew all about what had happened with

Kate. She could remember the accident happening, it had been big local news. And she said basically what everyone else had said, give her time. And Adam knew all about Wendy. Her divorce from her cheating husband, her kids, her grandchildren. Her love of golf and of the golf club which had resulted in her working in the bar there a few times a week. The sale of the marital home and her moving into the wonky walled house she was now residing in.

On paper they shouldn't have been friends even. Adam was in his early 30's, Wendy in her fifties; Adam hadn't asked at which point of her fifties she was at. But she looked good for her age, probably because of all the golf she played. He liked that she was a party animal and didn't take life too seriously, a bit like he had been years ago, without the drugs and the petty theft.

And even though they were close from the onset of him arriving at her house to work, they didn't do the whole flirt thing. It was like they had skipped the frivolous stage and moved straight to friendship. Adam liked it. Friends were something he didn't have a lot of. Not the type that would keep him on the straight and narrow.

Adam worked at Wendy's house for a week. She popped in and out all of the time. Sometimes she had been playing golf, or she had been to work or sometimes just out with her friends. Each time she came in she either brought him a pasty or a cake depending on what time of the day it was, but always with a smile on her face and a story to tell. Adam found himself drawn to her.

Wendy hadn't had the easiest of times. Her husband had dumped her for his much younger secretary, they'd had something going on for years she said. But he had left and married the secretary and now had a couple of little kids to go with the two he had with Wendy. But she didn't seem to be bitter about it. She even laughed saying that if anything, Keith; her ex-husband had cheated on his secretary, because right up until the very end, he had been all over Wendy. His lust for her had never waned. If he had been so in love with his secretary then he should have left Wendy well alone, she said at that point she probably wouldn't have noticed. She had a new love of her own – golf!

Adam felt something stirring when Wendy was telling him all of this. It had been so long since he had been affectionate with Kate and he had not so much have glanced in any other female's direction unless it involved tea and biscuits.

But Wendy was oozing with sex appeal. Not just in that moment but since the moment he had met her. Her lust for life, her laugh especially when she was telling him a funny story. There was just something about her. But the circled wallpaper was on the wall now and they both laughed and said that instead of it looking wonky, it now felt like they were locked in a big bottle of champagne. Wendy loved it. Adam said it was like her, she had made her living room an extension of herself, it was full of fizz. Adam saw the look on her face. Lust.

And then it was gone and Wendy rummaged in her bag until she found her purse and handed over payment for the painting and decorating to Adam in crisp £20 notes.

As Adam began to clear all of his equipment away into his van, a wave of sadness washed over him, Wendy had been a little ray of sunshine while he existed in the purgatory he existed in while he waited for Kate to decide whether she wanted or didn't want him. He was going to miss Wendy and somehow hoped that Wendy would message him now and again.

Just as he was about to drive away, he saw Wendy coming running out of the house. He wound down the window and Wendy said she just wanted to thank him, she loved her living room and like the fact that he had said that it reminded him of her. What about the hallway and stairs?? Could he come back and work him magic there too??

Ten minutes later he was driving towards home. The sadness diminished and a smile on his face. The hallway and stairs had been given a lick of paint not that long ago, he had been up and down the stairs enough to the loo to recognise something newly painted. If she wanted them decorated it was more to do with seeing Adam than getting her feng shui on the stairs. For some reason the thought of going back to Wendy's made him happier than he had been in weeks.

The messages started as soon as he got home. It was nice to have someone interested in him and not his decorating skills, because sadly apart from Wendy, that was the only type of messages he received. Kate remained very much absent. Wendy told him to keep the faith. What else could he do??

It was another three weeks before he went back to Wendy's to start decorating the stairs. During that time there had been hundreds and hundreds of messages. Wendy was just so easy to talk to, he told her about his life before his granddad died, his life after his granddad and then prison and beyond. Wendy had children of her own, she understood all about the pressures, said hers had been lucky because there had always been money off their dad and time off her! Wendy told him of the joy ride she had been on since she found herself single in her 50's, the men she had slept with, the ones that tried to sleep with her even though in many cases she played golf with their wives! It was a warts and all type of relationship. Adam had never had a friend like that before, male or female and certainly not with Kate. Kate had only ever been with Adam, she wouldn't and couldn't understand about how having a one-night stand made you feel. Good and bad.

There were so many layers to Wendy and Adam's friendship.

And as soon as he saw her again, the old stirrings were there. He was in no doubt that they were going to sleep together. She was older than him, a lot older than him but this wasn't about age, it was about something else. It was about trusting someone so much that you wanted to give them your everything. Wendy obviously felt the same way because within half an hour of him being back in her house, they were in her bed.

Wendy was as vivacious in the bedroom than she

was in life. She had no hang ups about her body and Adam saw no reason why she should ever have to have. In Wendy's words it was a joy ride.

Later there was no awkwardness. Adam worked, Wendy went to play golf only to turn up a few hours later with a cake to go with his afternoon tea.

They messaged when he wasn't with her, they had sex when they wanted to and they became the very best of friends. Adam did feel twinges of guilt when he thought about Kate. He had somehow reverted to type. But where was she? Where had Kate been all these weeks?? All these months??

This time when he finished the painting and decorating and Wendy had paid him in £20 notes again there was no need for her to magic him another room to decorate. They would still be seeing each other. Whatever it was they had going on it was good. Friends and lovers.

And then Kate got back in touch. Firstly she messaged and then she called and in his heart of hearts Adam was over the moon. He told Wendy about Kate, she said he must go and meet her, so he did. And Adam and Kate began courting again. It was a slow burn. The truth of it was she had hurt him. That was the second time she had rejected him when in reality he should have been by her side helping her through her ordeals.

And all the time he was on his new courtship with Kate, he continued to have a relationship with Wendy. He just wasn't ready to give her up. She knew everything about him, she knew about Kate and she was still prepared to be there for him. She would laughingly say why would she give up her toy boy, but there was more to it than that. They had something. It was just something that they just wanted to keep for themselves.

Even when Kate and Adam started spending nights together; he continued his relationship with Wendy. When he moved back into the house with Kate; he continued his relationship with Wendy. When Covid 19 arrived with lockdown restrictions; he continued his relationship with Wendy. If anything in that time it was easier to spend some time with her. Kate worked and he was left to his own devices a lot, so he would meet up with Wendy somewhere and they would walk and talk. And of course, the messages continued.

Wendy even managed to secure some painting and decorating work for Adam at the golf course, the 19th hole had a brand-new face lift and of course Wendy was on hand to help.

When Kate and Adam decided that they would get married, Adam and Wendy decided that they would part. It was a bittersweet time. Adam felt so sad without his phone pinging with messages from Wendy, he missed their talks and he missed her body. But it was the right time, he needed to be focused on Kate and the wedding.

It was lovely, Kate was lovely and it was the best of days. The day was tinged with sadness for the people who weren't there. Their names were said a lot during the service and every time they were Adam would add Wendy to the list. Adam missed her.

But he was a married man and he loved Kate. The trouble was that he loved Wendy too. He maybe even loved Wendy more. Wendy had never hurt him, she had never cast him aside and as much as it was that he had made his bed and he had to lie in it, he wasn't sure that he would keep his end of the bargain with Wendy and just get on with his life with Kate.

Adam did try though. For months and months it was just Adam and Kate. They were good, they were happy because she was happy. They had a good life together. But it wasn't enough, he needed to see Wendy. Adam needed to see that the fantasy woman that he had in his head was real or was she just simply a fantasy. A fling blown out of all proportion.

So, Adam texted Wendy. It took her three days to reply. She said that she was sorry, that she had been away on a golfing weekend, but Adam knew that she was lying. Even if she had been away she would have her phone with her. She had just been playing for time. But she agreed that he could go around and see her.

There is little of the Adam Mitchell of 10 years earlier. Kate and Adam are still together. Happy!! But there is still little of the Adam Mitchell of 10 years earlier and that is the little that continues to have a relationship with Wendy…

Does a leopard really change its spots????

'No matter how much a snake sheds skin. It's still a snake.'
Anon

4

Penny Dreadful

Rosie Sydney never touched £10 note HE75229564. Adam Mitchell had lied when he said he had handed the note over when he paid for a round of drinks in the bar where Rosie not only worked now and then, but lived with her parents. Adam didn't even pay for the round, his friend did; he lost £10 note HE75229564 on a dog!

But Rosie's story was told anyway. She was interesting and so was her story. Brought up in the Grey Goose pub which was situated on the outskirts of Newcastle, it was popular because it was cheaper than the City Centre and always had something going on to draw in the patrons.

It was said to be haunted, Rosie said she had never seen the ghost like figure of Penny Lord, the Grey Goose's first landlady, but others had. Allegedly she was a regular in the gents toilets. But maybe the apparition was more due to the spirits drank that the spirits of landladies past. But the stories would always keep coming. Ashen faced men telling tales of someone kissing their cheeks and running a finger down their spines as they stood at the urinals.

Ghosthunters had been in with their equipment; some even stayed all night, long after the pub had closed its doors, but there had never been anything. If Penny Lord did hang out in the gents; she played a game of hide and seek when the mood took her.

As for Rosie she was still living at the pub with her mam and dad. But they were on a countdown. It was time for her mam and dad to retire and after almost 30 years, they were going to go and live in a normal house with an upstairs and downstairs. Rosie could never remember having lived in a house before.

Rosie did think about getting a place of her own. She had talked about it a lot with her mam and dad, her work colleagues, punters in the bar, school mams, school dads. Anyone really!! But anyone who knew Rosie Sydney knew that it was all just smoke and mirrors, there was no way that she would strike out on her own with her little boy, Anthony. She had it far too cushy living with her mam and dad. Something that would only improve when they didn't have the ties of running the Grey Goose too.

After Rosie's marriage broke down, which again was no surprise to anyone except for Rosie, she did have a slight change of mindset. But it hadn't lasted.

You see Rosie Sydney was a chatterbox. Well not so much a chatterbox, more of an orator. She tended to talk at people. Poor John, her husband hadn't stood a chance. They had been childhood sweethearts according to Rosie, to John; Rosie was a guardian who kept the bullies at bay when his sexuality became something that he could no longer hide. In the beginning John thought it was just a friendship, Rosie thought it was a relationship and what Rosie thought usually became the reality of a situation.

Unfortunately, the reason that John was being ridiculed for by his school friends, Rosie didn't see. She thought his gratitude was something else and within no time, they became 'boyfriend and girlfriend'.

It was a situation that mild mannered John Sydney could not get out of. And so began his double life. And their life as the odd couple. Rosie talked and John didn't. Rosie certainly wore the trousers. Before he knew it John was moved into the flat above the Grey Goose with Rosie and a wedding date had been set. Rosie always all consuming, she was blinkered and didn't see anything beyond her nose. Luckily for John, his job kept him away for the best part of a week, usually he would just have to be with Rosie on weekends. In his mind every time he returned to the Grey Goose it would be the right time to tell Rosie that he didn't want to marry her. But there was never chance and before he knew it he had a wife.

And then she was pregnant and if Rosie had taken the time to look at her husband, she would have seen that he was suffocating. But of course, she didn't look at him. The baby was her new project and even if John had tried to tell Rosie how he was feeling she wouldn't have listened to him. She had no idea who the man was she was married to.

When the baby's due date arrived, John was staying at

the Grey Goose full time. It wasn't that he didn't want to be a father, it was more the fact that he could not imagine living as mam and dad and baby with Rosie. He cared about Rosie, he did, he loved her! But he loved her as a friend. The physical side of his relationship with Rosie made him feel ill. He was so grateful that when Rosie had decided that she wanted a baby, it had happened quickly. It was a blessing in disguise really because then he had an excuse not to have sex with Rosie; what if they hurt the baby?? For once Rosie listened and that was the end of any shenanigans.

The night that Rosie went into labour it had all become too much for John and it came to a head.

John Sydney gained a son and lost his wife.

He only wished that Rosie could have seen John before it all got to that point. If only she had listened to the bullies at school and the reason that they were bullying him. But she hadn't and when the truth of it all came out Rosie took it all badly.

You see when John Sydney wasn't living with Rosie, he was living with Will. Will was the love of John's life. He had met him while he was working away, they had met and instantly clicked. But John hadn't worked away for a long time, realistically since the marriage. John would leave the Grey Goose on a Monday morning, go to work and then return to the home of Will until he had to make his way back to his wife on a Friday evening.

The couple of weeks that he spent with Rosie before the birth of the baby were the longest he had ever spent away from Will. It was too much and he lost the plot. He had got so far into the pregnancy without any major meltdowns, but that was because he had Will holding his hand. Without Will it was all too much.

So the meltdown happened, the baby was born and John returned to the Grey Goose, sat down and talked with Rosie's mam and dad, who were surprisingly supportive of his decision to leave Rosie and his new born son, he packed up his belongings and made his way back to Will.

But they had Anthony Declan Sydney to consider and something needed to be sorted out. It was over a month before Rosie saw John again. By then she was over the shock that her husband was actually gay and was totally consumed with Anthony. But she was quieter; less talking at and more talking to. A lesson learned maybe.

Co-parenting had worked out well. Anthony knew no different. He had a mam and two dads. Rosie had divorced John and then a couple of years later he had married Will. Rosie, Anthony and Rosie's mam and dad had been at the wedding. Rosie had thought that her wedding to John was better but she would say that; that was Rosie.

Anthony was a lovely young lad. Having been brought up in a pub, he was sociable and was a firm favourite with all the regulars. At 8 he was a bit on the quiet side like his dad, but looks wise he was the spit of his mam. He was spoilt off all of his parents and his grandma and granddad but not so much in a materialistic way, more time. Everyone had time for him.

Rosie was very much still single.

When her marriage first collapsed, she had gone out with one of the regulars for a few months, but that had phased out, Rosie wasn't really ready for a new man in her life, she already had one in the shape of Anthony.

All her attention was on him. She took him to playgroups and toddler groups and by the time he started nursery school, she had resorted somewhat to type and was back to talking at people, usually telling all the other mams and dads how much better Anthony was at doing things than their child. People tended to avoid her when they could. But not Anthony; he seemed to win everyone over so although it pained many of Anthony's friends' mams and dads to invite Anthony to parties and such like because of his overbearing mam; they still invited him and just put up with Rosie and her bragging.

When lockdown came Rosie found that without anyone to talk to beyond her mam, dad and Anthony, she was quite lonely.

So she joined an internet dating site and set off in search of someone who was like minded. Like so many things in her life, it became all-consuming and each day when she finished work in the makeshift office she had made in her bedroom and Anthony was sorted and happy, she would scour the website in search of her Mr Right.

As restrictions lifted Rosie found herself on lots of walking dates. There wasn't really anything else to do on a first date, there were no restaurants or cinemas. She loved the walking but the men weren't for her. Or more to the point she wasn't really for them!!

To Rosie it was a puzzle. She wasn't bad looking. With all the walking she had shred the extra lbs she had put on during the first lockdown and even though she must have had more than 15 dates, they had all been first dates and a second had never materialised. The promise of 'I'll message you' never happened.

But by the time the majority of the restrictions were lifted and the Grey Goose opened up properly her love life took a back seat and it was all hands-on pump when the customers came through the doors in their droves.

It was all work, work, work and Anthony. There were so many people to talk to, it had been so long since she had an audience that wasn't her family or a would-be boyfriend. It was exhilarating. New customers flirted with her, she loved it. Surely there would be someone walk through the Grey Goose doors who would be right for her and want to see her more than once. So she cancelled her subscription to the singles website and kept a keen eye on the pub door for a would be suitor.

And then came Rosie's mam and dad's bomb shell. They wanted to retire; the whole Covid 19 Lockdowns and restrictions had made their minds up. It was a younger person's game they said. Rosie cried. She loved the Grey Goose, the flat, the people. She even went so far as to offer to take over the tenancy and just pack her job in the computer shop. Her mam and dad wouldn't hear of it. It was no life for a single woman with a small boy. Rosie had no argument back. They were right; while she had grown up there herself there had been many a night when she was little that she had been left up in the flat on her own. She knew her mam and dad were just downstairs and could be with her in minutes, but still. She didn't want that life for Anthony if the truth be known.

So Rosie did what she did best and became obsessed with finding somewhere for herself and Anthony to live. She worked out all of the sums and when the realisation hit that even if she got herself a small two bedroomed house and taking into account the money that she got for Anthony off John; there would be very little money left even for food. There was only one thing for her to do, go wherever her mam and dad went.

And here we are 6 months later. Rosie's mam and dad are almost finished their notice period. The new tenants are about to come in and get the feel for the Grey Goose before the Brand family departed for their new life.

It is going to be strange for all of them. They have a lovely new 4 bedroomed house to move in to. As far removed from the shabby flat they have lived in for decades, that in itself filled them all with excitement. But how they will all cope when they don't have a bar to escape to. Rosie has no idea what she will do when Anthony goes to stay with John and Will every other weekend and whereas normally she would go into the bar and help out, chat to customers and listen to the band playing, now there would be nowhere to go.

Rosie had never really thought much about it before

but beyond her job and the Grey Goose and her family, she has very little. No best friend, no friends really, no hobbies! There was a void opening and every time she thought about it; it seemed to get bigger and that filled her with dread. She adored her mam and dad but what would they do when they didn't have work? Her mam and dad talked of holidays and had even gone as far as booking a cruise for a few months' time when they were all settled into the house. But still!

With the call for last orders imminent, Rosie knows that things have to change in her life. She needs to find herself a social life. Her biggest fear is that because she knows no different she will find herself sitting on the other side of the bar in the Grey Goose! Her mam and dad won't be around for ever, Anthony will come to a point where he doesn't need her as much and then what?? For the first time in her life Rosie Sydney knew that she was going to have to take a good long look at herself. Before she could move forward she needed to look back because unlike other women her age, beyond the obvious she had nothing …

'When you talk, you are only repeating what you already know. But if you listen, you may learn something new.'

Dalai Lama

5

Hand to Mouth

Debs Johnston only had £10 note HE75229564 fleetingly. When Adam Mitchell had lost the £10 on a dead cert of a greyhound which went like a rocket, so fast that it fell over at the first bend. The dog tumbled and so did Adam Mitchell's life, for then anyway. Debs had taken the note and placed it into the cash register at the bookies where she worked.

But someone had a bit of luck, almost a grands worth, and £10 note HE75229564 was out of the till and into the hands of Jake, one of the bookies regulars. But as often happened, the punter would tip the cashier, it sometimes felt to Debs that the winners thought they would jinx themselves if they didn't see the cashier ok. So Deb's gratefully took the tip off Jake, it was £10 HE75229564.

Debs lived very much hand to mouth. A single mam with 3 growing boys, money was always on the scarce side. There was always something they wanted; to eat, to wear or somewhere they wanted to go. For Debs it was relentless and although her hours at the bookies was almost full time and to be fair a good hourly rate; there was still not enough money to go around, every day she juggled.

But she had healthy and mainly happy kids, they saw her doing her best and she had the support of her mam and dad who stepped in to help with childcare, the odd bit of money, but mainly a steadying hand on the rocky boat Debs called her life.

£10 note HE75229564 was lucky for Jake in the bookies, it turned out to be lucky for Debs too. It changed her life. Not in a massive way, she didn't up sticks and move into some big swanky house somewhere. But it did make a difference.

On the night she got the tip off Jake she made her way to the convenience shop over the road from the bookies. She tended to shop daily, it was more cost effective; if she bought food for the coming days then it just wasn't cost effective. The boys would eat their way through it, and she would end up having to buy double. So more was the habit was to buy daily for the next day and a little extra for the boys and there endless bouts of hunger.

Anyway that night, with a little extra in her purse and some savvy shopping in the clearance section of the shop, she had everything she needed and a couple of quid spare. On a whim and hoping that maybe some of Jakes luck had rubbed off on her, she bought a scratch card, something that she didn't do very often. A scratch card that she promptly forgot about when she got home and didn't think about scratching until a few days later when she was clearing off the top of her fridge.

The run of luck had continued and the scratch card

turned out to be a winner. £6,666!!! Not a massive amount in some people's books. But to Debs it literally changed her life forever.

The catalogues and doorstep loan payments had been paid off, no more high interest weekly payments for Debs. If she or the boys needed anything she had managed to save for them. It was a new and liberating thing for Debs, a little nest egg or rainy day fund. She had always loved her job, but it had been a means to an end when she knew that the money for every hour she worked was already spoken for. It was soul destroying. After her win, Debs began to have a different perspective about her work. It became a job and not a cash cow.

As the boys grew and her work life didn't depend so much on childcare, Debs began to look at what her job was all about. Gambling. In truth she couldn't knock it. If she hadn't gambled on a scratch card then she would never had won the money. But working in the bookies she saw the hard core and more destructive side of gambling and the addiction she became.

Almost every day she saw someone lose what they couldn't afford. And not just money. Wives, husband, families, employment. Gambling was the biggest buzz when people were winning, but flip side was something else. The cash machine in the corner of the shop was forever having to be filled up with cash and when it became a more credit and debit card environment, the punters were done for.

The bookies was part of a national chain. Deb's shop was a small fish in a very big pond. Everything was the best of. Décor, televisions, bandits, even the complimentary teas and coffees were the best of brands. The bookie always won and the profits were there for all to see.

But it all troubled Debs. How many lives had she watched being destroyed? She knew about the £10 note that brought her her own good fortune. She also knew where it came from Adam Mitchell. He had blown £10 HE75229564 right in front of her eyes; on a dead cert greyhound that was probably sent to the glue factory the minute it botched up its race. She also remembered how losing the money had sent Adam Mitchell on a journey that led him straight into prison. At the time it had really upset Debs, Adam was a nice lad who was in the wrong crowd and in a situation, he didn't seem to be able to get out of. Prison changed him. For the good. These days Adam Mitchell was known for his flourishing painting and decorating business and not his shady life. Debs had even employed him when her mam and dad moved into an old peoples bungalow and it needed sprucing up. It had been good to see how well his life had turned out.

Adam Mitchell was one of the luckier ones. Others turned to drink and drugs. But there is always a straw that breaks the camel's back. One thing that made Deb's question why she was working at the bookies, basically being paid for other people's misfortune. Obviously she wasn't alone, her company alone employed thousands, but when one of the young mam's who came into the bookies regularly every morning to drink the free coffee and play on the bandit machines tried to kill herself, Debs knew that she wanted to do something else. The young mam had survived, but it had put the care of her children at risk; rumour had it she had spent all of the money out of her children's account, lost the lot. And that was Deb's last straw.

Debs handed in her notice. With no clear plan on what she would do next, she gave 3 months. She hadn't needed to, she could have got away with a month, but she liked her manager, she knew that the shifts that she did were the more undesirable ones and be hard to fill and theoretically thought it would give her time to think about what next.

£10 HE75229564 had also brought her Craig. To Debs he was the love of her life, but Craig wasn't big on endearments and although they had said 'love you' to each other, it wasn't something that was said very often. Usually in the throws of passion, but it was felt.

One of the first things Debs had bought with her lucky scratch card win was a huge washing machine. The machine had arrived and so had Craig. It wasn't an immediate thing, though Debs was haunted by him in her dreams after he had installed the machine and it was by pure chance or was it fate that brought them back into each other's lives. But even then, it had been a slow burn. Debs had never met anyone like him. He was a deep thinker, an old soul and often illusive. But that hadn't been because he had been getting up to something with someone else or anything; he just liked to be on his own.

They persevered though and even though he was still

given to going off on his own for a few days, he would keep in touch and Debs didn't take it personally. It was just her lovely Craig. The boys liked him, her mam and dad liked him; and Debs loved him unconditionally.

Craig was supportive in her decision to hand in her notice. Told her not to worry, there would be a job somewhere that would suit her. He had never liked her working at the bookies; allegedly his granddad had been a gambling man and his nan had lived a hell of a life with him, so he had strong views on the unscrupulous profession of being a bookmaker. But for Debs it was all a bit of a worry. She checked for vacancies on the job centre website; there was nothing that caught her eye. There was time though.

But then Covid arrived and everything changed. For everyone.

Suddenly she was at home 24/7 and though in the first instance it was bliss; no work, no school just endless sunny days of doing nothing. It didn't last. With 3 boys in the house who were all not used to not seeing their mates or having the freedom to come and go, it very quickly became a war zone and Debs found she was playing referee more and more.

Even her mam and dad not popping in and out was an alien experience for Debs. She had never not seen them almost every day and even though she would go and sit in their garden with them, it wasn't the same. Craig did the same. He would come and while a couple of hours away in her garden; they didn't touch; they didn't think that they were allowed to, no one really knew what was going on, but Craig was a stickler for the rules so when the 2 metre rule came in, he stuck to it. It was frustrating; thank God for Facetime!

Debs continued to shop at Mr Singh's, but even that didn't require a visit, she would text in what she wanted for herself and more often her mam and dad. They would send her how much she owed and she would leave the cash on the doorstep or transfer the amount to them in time for the delivery. It truly was the strangest of times.

Like everyone else; she watched the Press Conferences at 5pm each daily religiously and clapped her little heart out every Thursday evening at 8pm. What else could she do?

Workwise she was unsure what was happening. Debs was officially on her notice, but with the shop closed she waited patiently to see if she would continue to get paid. She had the generic emails sent to everyone about the assurance of her next monthly pay, but still there was only another month or so left of her notice and then what.

Clarity came in the shape of a telephone call from her area manager. Kim Renick had worked for years at the bookies in the next town. Debs and Kim had met lots of times when she had come to cover in Debs shop, but then she had gone for promotion and had been flying ever since. So after all the pleasantries were over and Kim explained about the new Furlough Scheme that was being rolled out by the Government; Kim got down to the nitty gritty.

Basically, Kim didn't want to lose Debs. She stated hardworking reliable staff were hard to come by so truly didn't want to lose such a valued member of the team.

Debs told her why she felt that the position was something she found so conflicting; the Adam Mitchell's; the young mam. That Debs felt somewhat responsible for other people's misfortunes.

Kim said she knew how Debs had been feeling, it had been fed back to her when she had handed in her notice and it was something that Kim had wanted to address. So, she had gone up the line to her manager and so on and so forth and the upshot of it all was that they would like Debs to retract her notice and they would like to help her train as an addiction's counsellor; specifically gambling addictions. It was something that they had never considered before and even though they looked like they would be shooting themselves in the foot; they had a duty of care towards their customers and their staff. Debs would be, if she was willing to accept the position; the start of many. They wanted to be front runners in the business; maybe they would lose customers but that was far better than what some of their customers stood to lose.

Debs was gobsmacked. She had not seen that coming; to be honest she thought the conversation would have resulted in her job being terminated earlier than expected.

Kim said she would email all of the correspondence with regard to enrolling on to the first stage course and they would take it from there. If she was prepared to do the course on-line from home while the shop was closed; then her full new salary would be assured. Kim asked Debs to think it over.

It was a no brainer. Debs had been looking for something; this was her something. This would allow her to have her work history and get her teeth into something she felt passionately about. She was going to be the pilot scheme for the whole company; nationally! Debs said she didn't have to think about it; that she would look out for the email and they would take it from there!

And that is what happened. It hadn't been easy. Debs wasn't as computer savvy as most so it took a while to sort through just doing the application process; but the boys had helped; and slowly she began to make her way through the modules; sometimes with a fight with the boys for the most decent laptop they had when they boys had Zoom calls with school; but they did it. Somehow watching their mam work hard; when theoretically she could have just been sitting in the garden with the neighbours, made the boys dig in a bit deeper. They seemed calmer and the fighting at the beginning of the pandemic wasn't half as bad as they made their way out of the summer and towards winter.

Even when the shop reopened and Debs went back to work; she remained focused on her studies; applied some of her new found knowledge to one or two of the customers; something she wouldn't have done months earlier; then she would have just frowned or shook her head. No, she was confident enough to question customers if she felt there was a need to. Not in an intrusive way; just a chat over one of the free cups of coffee and the chance to divert someone away from a mistake that she was sure they were going to make.

Craig was really proud of her; that she had done something about something she felt passionately about and even when he was allowed to have sleepovers again; her focus remained.

Nowadays Debs is a fully qualified gambling counsellor; employed by the same bookmakers she had worked for years for. The pilot scheme had worked; the company gained recognition within the business as being a responsible gambling institution and Debs and Craig had even attended an awards ceremony where both Debs and Kim had received awards.

It had worked so well that each area of the United Kingdom had its own gambling counsellor; all tucked nicely under Debs wing. Just like Kim before her; once she started on the promotion ladder, she too had flown.

The boys were now all grown up. Declan worked for the same bookmakers as his mam; but he worked in the IT department, looking after all of the technology in all of the North East shops; he had moved in with his girlfriend and in a few months' time; Debs was going to be a grandma. Rory still lived at home with Debs; most of the time. He too had a long term girlfriend and he tended to spend a lot of time at her mam and dad's house; though Debs still did his washing and they both tended to rock up at her house at silly o'clock when they had been in town; cheaper taxi ride apparently.

And little; though not so little and the tallest of all her boys; Jasper was at Leeds University. He thought that he might like to be a teacher; but with only being in his second year, there was plenty of time to make his mind up. He came home when he could and seemed to be living his best life as a student.

Debs felt that she really should have empty nest syndrome; but she didn't.

Craig would come and stay over once or twice a week; or she would go and stay at his house; the same house that he had bought off his mam a few years earlier. Being a father of teenagers, he was run ragged off his kids and these days was not half as elusive as he had been in the first few years. Debs was his go to woman; what didn't she know about teenagers.

And then there was her job. It was ever evolving and after securing her position as a qualified counsellor; Debs had taken the plunge and learned to drive. How had she never driven before? Even going to Leeds to see Jasper was not off limits.

Ironically as it was. One little scratch card changed Debs life. It was a story she would tell customers; how the scratch card she had bought because someone had been lucky and handed over her a ten pound a note as a tip after a big win. It had been £10 note HE75 229564. The same ten pound not that Adam Mitchell had lost on a dead cert dog only an hour so early. An action that sent him spiralling to prison but ultimately straightened out his life once and for all.

Life is full of luck; good and bad. But its knowing when to cut your losses or quit while your ahead is the name of the game.

Debs hasn't bought a scratch card since her winning one. That had been enough. She was happy and healthy; had a job she now loved, her boys and of course Craig, who she would never had met if she hadn't won the money, bought her new washing machine and encountered her fit fitter!!

'In gambling the many must lose in order that the few may win'
George Bernard Shaw

6

Look After the Pennies and the Pounds Will Look After Themselves

Ravi Singh had run the local corner shop for over 20 years. He had been the recipient of £10 note HE75 229564 when Debs Johnston had used it to pay for her groceries and her lucky scratch card. Mr Singh had been happy for her; she was one of his regular customers, always had a ready smile and made time to ask after him and his family. Even after she had her lucky windfall, Debs remained a faithful customer, as were so many.

The shop had been good to Mr Singh and his family. His wife; Mani and he had lived in the upstairs flat with their two children Kal and Mela. It had been their home and haven and although they worked hard; they'd had a good life.

But the long hours and the worry had taken its toll on Ravi and Mani; even with the arrival of his brother and his entourage and the extra pairs of hands that they brought; it had been tough. They had all lived together in the spacious flat above the shop and even though it was a good size, with the onset of covid 19 and the restrictions that brought to the extended family of 9; it was too small and even before it was officially stated by the government that Lockdown was a law; Kal and Mela had moved out. Kal to stay with some friends and Mela moved into her boyfriend's house.

It had broken their mother's heart.

But Mr Singh understood why they had gone. They had been brought up in a much more liberal way than that of their uncle and his family in the South; and whereas Mr and Mrs Singh could adapt; Kal and Mela wouldn't, and they all knew that it would result in family feuds.

So the children had left and the dynamics of the shop took on a yet another shape as they worked their way around what the Covid 19 Lockdown and all of the rules and regulations that they threw at them. All the while Mani ate her way through her unhappiness and her ever growing waistline and ill health continued. It got so bad that she became virtually housebound.

Then there was his own ill health. Though he was still as trim as he had been in his youth; his knees were buggered. All of the hours of standing in the shop; running up and down to the stock room and up and down the stairs to the flat had caused his knees to simply wear away; the first knee replacement had been scheduled for April; the first April of lockdown and the operation had been cancelled. So he continued to pop the pills and had as many hot baths and cold ice packs as he could muster.

But they muddled through. Thank God for Sandhu really, he had picked up the slack, he had been the one that suggested they up their delivery service and bought a couple of extra vans and he was the one that made sure that all the screens, sanitisers and signage was in place to allow customers to come into the shop if they so wished. Mani controlled the orders on her mobile phone in the shop and they all chipped in downstairs; sorting the orders and setting up delivery routes. It was hard work, but to be honest, they shop was thriving. It had never made so much money.

Then against all the odds, Mani caught Covid. For the life of them they had no idea how that had happened; she barely left the flat. It could only have been one of the other family members. But whereas the rest all remained well, Mani was oh so poorly. Her health was so poor that she had nothing to fight the virus with and when after there was no improvement after two weeks; an ambulance crew came and took her into hospital.

Ravi Singh was distraught. He had never spent more than a night away from his wife of almost 40 years. It was more than that though. It was the way she was taken away. The ambulance crew arrived covered in protective clothing; they almost looked like a bomb squad and Mani was a bomb that would go off at any minute.

And then she was gone. Ravi didn't see her again for almost 3 months. There was no visiting allowed and for the first few months Mani had been so poorly; even seeing her on a Facetime call arranged by the nurses was upsetting. Watching his wife labour to catch breath and not be with her was horrific; if Ravi hadn't been so tired with all the additional work they were doing and the constant pills he was popping he wouldn't have slept for the worry.

Mani eventually began to rally. By the time Ravi was able to go into the hospital and see her she was a shadow of the woman that had been stretchered out of their little flat. The weight had dropped off her and even though it was better than she was no longer classed as clinically obese; she now seemed to have the body and health of a woman 20 years older than her. She looked 80; even the beautiful peppered black hair was now almost white and the doctors talked of something called long covid; but no one knew if that was even a thing. It just seemed that Mani was worn out. Old before her years.

There was talk of a care home for Mani so that she could recuperate. Ravi didn't want that. The money it would cost alone was eye watering, but it was more than that; he didn't want someone else looking after his wife. It wasn't what his family did. They looked after their own. But he couldn't do both. He couldn't be in the shop 24/7 and be there for Mani. Even with the help of the rest of the live in family and Kal and Mela it would be too much.

It was a worry. But at least he could get in to see his wife now; suited up like one of the bomb disposal team that had taken Mani away from him. Each time he saw her she looked a little better; the oxygen mask was constantly in her hand and sometimes if she got over excited she lost her breath. How could Ravi even begin to give her the care she needed.

It was Kal who came up with some hope. Party loving, smart Kal who was now as English as they came. Who was into his 30s and still very much a man about town. But he was enterprising; he always had been. Much smarter than his parents could ever have been; happy to help in the shop but there would be no way that he would have ever worked the hours his mam and dad did.

And it seemed that his friends were of a similar ilk; because with all the businesses going to the wall during the pandemic; Kal and his old university friend and business partner Ash had swooped in and bought some property. Ravi really was blown away when the deal had been done and Kal had taken his dad to see what they had bought and the blueprint of what they would be doing with it.

As the crow flew it wasn't far away from the shop. But whereas the shop was surrounded by terraced houses and housing estate; The Dairy as it was known; was perched on the top of a hill with only fields and fields for a view. The Dairy had gone out of business a few months earlier and the dairy itself along with all of the storage areas; offices and houses that were scattered within the property had been sold as a job lot at a knock down price.

The plan was to make a restaurant along with hotel accommodation and one of the fields to be a gite village which seemed to be all of the rage these days and a 9 hole golf course. The investment had been secured and the builders were due in any day to make a start on the conversion. The first building that was to be spruced up was a little cottage that nestled on the road on the way up the hill. Kal said he wanted his mam and dad to live there; it he had said had been the dealbreaker.

For once in his life Ravi Singh was speechless.

The cottage needed refurbishing, but Ravi could see Mani and him living there. No stairs to be climbed; for both of them. They would be able to sit in the garden with little effort; maybe even venture on little walks; Lord knew they could both do with it. It was the solution he had been looking for; Mani could live a better life there. No nursing home; no shop; just some peace and quiet and the chance to both live a better life.

And that's exactly how it all happened in the end.

Mani and Ravi moved into their cottage. They had lived there almost two years now. Mani is still classed as having long covid; she had to be careful not to catch coughs and colds as more often than not it takes her off her feet and she ends up in her bed for a week or two.

Ravi handed over the day to day running of the shop to his brother Sandhu and his family; but he and Mani still gleamed a good living from it; more than enough to contribute to Kal's flourishing business; that what their families did. They all helped each other.

Ravi was even able to take the time to have a knee replaced one year and the other the next. He was like a new man; he could walk up the hill to The Dairy no trouble these days and would happily help out in the kitchen or bar. It had only been open a matter of months but was already proving to be popular and with the opening of the gites in the summer it was exciting times for the Singh family.

£10 note HE75 229564 didn't make much difference to Ravi Singh's life. It had been in and out of his till as quick as a flash; that had been the nature of the business. But he knew it's value; he knew that if you worked hard and looked after your money you could provide for your family. But he also learned that keeping healthy was worth more than any money. He knew that the years and years of looking after the pennies had almost put paid to Mani and his health. It had been Kal and his smarter way of working that had given them a better quality of life. But to Ravi it was swings and roundabouts; if he and Mani had not worked from dawn until dusk then Kal wouldn't have had the opportunities he had and then in turn what would have happened to him and Mani? it was something that often crossed his mind as he strode up the hill to The Dairy; what came first; the chicken or the egg???

'You Can't Enjoy Wealth if You're Not in Good Health.'
Anonymous

7

Worth Your Weight in Gold

For Susan Cole, £10 note HE75 229564 that she received in her change from Mr Singh was unimportant. More important were the 3 bottles of wine that she had bought on his special of 3 bottles for £10. The three bottles that she would drink that night when she had got back to the seclusion of her own home.

With the loss of her husband, Arnie; Susan had been left with only his mother as family. Betty! Whilst Arnie had been alive Susan and Betty had a very cold relationship, but when Arnie unexpectedly died, it had been Betty who had got Susan through the darkest of days.

Susan's friendship with Betty had been something that Susan would always cherish. It was a relationship that she never expected to have, a one she probably would never have had if Arnie had lived.

Arnie, her one and only love.

Abandoned by her parents, brought up by her grandma, Susan didn't have much of a family, but meeting and falling in love with Arnie had been all she could ever have wanted. A year after they met they married and Susan had the best 10 years of her life. She was loved and worshipped and cherished off Arnie. They travelled the world, had a nice house and even though they both worked hard, there was barely a cross word between them. Even when the children they had both talked about when they first married had not materialised, it didn't matter. They had each other.

But then he had gone and died on her and Susan felt the abandonment she had felt for the majority of her life return again.

Not that Susan ever let Betty know that. Her mother-in-law went above and beyond to make sure that there was also something for Susan to look forward to. Afternoon teas, trips to the theatre, mini breaks followed by holidays.

Then Betty left too. She didn't die. Not straightaway. It was a long slow painful demise. Dementia. Susan hardly noticed at first, it was just a few forgetful phone calls where Betty had called to tell her something and then she could call again twice or thrice telling her exactly the same thing. Or she would forget they were doing something and Susan would call around to collect her and she would still be sitting in her nightwear. Just little things.

Within months though it had taken hold and so had the wine.

Betty disappeared down a rabbit hole and Susan went with her.

As Betty's care became more and more demanding. Susan drank and drank. Her nightly one bottle was soon three and then she would add a few spirits into the mix.

Every night Arnie returned to the chair he used to sit in when he was an actual being and not a figment of Susan's drunken stupor. She would sit on his knee and tell him how she couldn't cope with life without him, that she couldn't cope with his mother and she would cry. Other nights the drink would take out her rage at him and she would throw her wine glass or wine bottle at him. How could he have left her.

In the cold light of morning, when Arnie had gone and the only remnant of him even being there the night before was the broken bottles and wine stains, Susan knew she wasn't coping. She had gone on the sick from her job at Police HQ and her days were made up of caring for Betty. Every day it got a little bit worse and every day Susan's need for a drink got earlier and earlier in the day. The whole situation was all consuming.

And then Betty died.

For a while there was only oblivion for Susan. Looking back she had no recollection of the funeral at all. Susan would always feel shame about that. As difficult the time before Betty's passing had been, she deserved the best version of Susan she could have had. Susan had no idea what version she had. The only consolation that Susan had was that there would have only been a few mourners.

Susan's wakeup call came in the shape of the estate agent, someone wanted to view Betty's house, it had been on the market so long Susan had forgotten it was even up for sale. But no one wanted to buy a house they could not view internally, and Betty had not been the most welcoming of hosts, now she was gone there was no excuse.

For the first time in months, Susan had to pull herself together and make sure that Betty's abandoned home was fit for viewing.

In a roundabout way it was the making of Susan.

The house was made good, the first prospective buyers bought it and Susan found that when she filled her days doing stuff, her thirst for alcohol was not so great.

Within weeks of the house selling, Susan decided that she would go back to work. A job that she had done almost all her adult life, her work colleagues were more her friends than associates and that again was another step on the road to recovery.

Almost a year after Betty died, Susan's life could not have looked more different. She had not quite knocked the drink on the head altogether, but she was only having one bottle a night, sometimes less. She had gained weight and she had taken the mammoth step of selling her marital home and buying a smaller new build.

Arnie had not gone with her to the new house. Now the only place Arnie could be found was in her memories and in her heart.

And she had a new love.

Gardening. It became the salve that helped heal her wounds. Planting and tending and watching something grow was her greatest pleasure. More so than the wine!

LAST NOTE

By the time the United Kingdom went into National Lockdown in March of 2020, Susan was content.

Susan loved her house. It was small, but it suited her fine. She had her garden; her neighbours were all lovely and some she now even classed as friends. She had splashed out on a small greenhouse so even through the winter she could keep her green fingers active. There was still a glass or two of wine each night, but she added lemonade nowadays and made it in to a longer drink, theoretically a glass of wine could last her all night if she diluted it down. The wine was no longer all consuming.

Arnie never ever materialised at the new house. She had never got herself into anywhere near the type of stupors that she had previously. The type that conjured her dead husband out of thin air. The type that drove her to a mighty rage at Arnie or an unquenchable thirst for more alcohol.

Susan's life was calm.

Even when the lockdown restricted her to the boundaries of her home, it didn't make her want to drink more alcohol. She pottered around, took herself on walks that she would never normally have opportunity to take. She walked past her old marital home; from the outside it looked the same, but she knew inside now homed a family of 6; the house would be alive.

Susan walked past Betty's house, only to find that the scaffolding that had gone up soon after the sale went through was still up and the house still seemed to remain unoccupied.

Work sent a computer and mobile phone to her home. The office would not be operating as was, but they could do what they could from home and very soon, Susan had made herself an office in the spare bedroom and her life took on a new rhythm.

As did every other person in the country; Susan watched the daily Downing Street updates religiously. She watched the numbers go up and up and knew that if there was anything she could do to help she would. But for the life of her, beyond clapping on her doorstep every Thursday night at 8pm and her job working for the Police; there was nothing.

It was a strange time. Susan felt like the world had hit the 'pause' button. From what she could make out, people were going back to basics. Family time, cooking, reading. It had been a long time since Susan had read a book, even when her neighbour Helen handed over a carrier bag stuff full of paperbacks, Susan thought they would just sit in her cupboard until the charity bags started arriving back through her door.

But one night, after her plants were watered and the sun was setting outside and the conservatory had a warm pink hue; Susan decided that maybe she might have a look at the books Helen had given her. She could not remember the last time she had actually read a book, probably in her teens; definitely not since she had met and lost Arnie.

Opening the cover of the first book, she was hooked.

Lockdown brought Susan some kind of peace that

she had never known. Yes the people she loved had abandoned her, but she knew that if he could, Arnie would be sitting in the chair opposite, laughing at her for crying at a book.

Somehow, she did not feel alone anymore. Susan felt content.

And by the time a vaccine had been found; Susan had volunteered to be a steward at one of the vaccination centres. She found a purpose in all of the madness of the Covid Pandemic.

Susan ushered the hoards and hoards of scared people attending the local health centre for their first vaccination. She made sure that they kept the 2-metre rule standing them on the purpose made yellow dots. Always with a smile on her face behind the mask and a cheery word of encouragement.

To be honest her vaccination had made her ill for two days, but she would never tell the patients that. If the country was ever going to get back to some sort of normality; then the majority would have to go through the vaccination centres.

For the next two years Susan worked when she could at the health centre; picking up shifts when she wasn't working. It became a way of life for her and she made some good friends. One of the volunteers; Ian started on the same day she did. They sat through the training together and when at the end of the day they started to walk home, it turned out that they lived on the same estate.

It became a regular occurrence that if they were

working at the health centre at the same time, they would take the walk together.

When Ian asked Susan if she maybe like to go for a walk on a day they weren't working, she panicked and said no.

Later, when she had read the same line in the book she was reading for about the 6th time, she kicked herself. Ian had only asked her to go for a walk, not run away and get married.

As she got ready for bed that night, she took a good long look at herself in the mirror, something she didn't do very often.

She was heading towards mid 40's but probably looked older. The grief and alcohol had aged her. Her hair was too long; she couldn't remember the last time she had been to the hairdressers. Maybe with the lifting of some restrictions she could book in and get it cut and coloured. She was sure if she looked closely enough there would be lots of grey hairs; it definitely needed doing. Her body wasn't so bad now. Having never had children her tummy was flat and her breasts were still pert. Her legs, lady garden and arm pits needed tending to. She had neglected herself so badly.

Ian asking her to go for a walk was maybe the kick up the arse she needed and vowed that when she got up in the morning she would call the hairdressers and get herself in the bath and sort out all her unwanted bits and bobs and then maybe even paint her toenails. Even if she never went for a walk with Ian, she needed to take better care of herself.

But Susan did go for a walk with Ian.

It was the start of a very slow burn relationship.

Ian was ten years older, but Susan thought he looked younger than her. He kept himself fit, usually with the gym and 5 a side football and golf, but during the pandemic he had walked a lot.

Susan wondered how he was still standing. Just as the country went into lockdown, his wife of 30 years left him. Susan thought that his wife's timing was very cruel. Ian said that she could not stand the thought of not seeing the person she had been seeing for however long and had gone. Ian thought he had seen it coming, but never knew how to talk about it to her. Susan couldn't understand that, but then she'd had a happy marriage.

Anyway, away she went and Ian had trundled on without her. He was a dad and a grandfather and seemed to be close to his children. He too was working from home and saw the volunteering job as chance to get out of the house. Ian was quite outdoorsy so took the whole lockdown thing badly, more than the absence of his wife.

After the first walk there were more. Susan found that she could open up to Ian. They walked and talked. She told him about her mam and dad leaving her with her grandma and never coming back for her. She told him of her grandma dying just after her 18th birthday. She told him about meeting Arnie, falling in love and marrying him. Ian was a good listener and if he was bored about hearing of all the places Susan and Arnie had travelled to; he never said. Some of the places he had been to himself.

Susan told him of Arnie's death. Of Betty friendship and then the demise of everything. Ian didn't judge. Just congratulated her on getting out the other side.

When Ian asked Susan to go on a little holiday, she faltered only for a second, if the last few years had taught her anything it was life was for living, so she said yes and off they went.

It was the first of many little jaunts.

When the vaccination roll out finished and they had more time on their hands, they began going to the pictures or theatre or out for meals.

Susan and Ian courted.

For Susan it was a very different to the courtship she'd had with Arnie. Then it had been Happy Ever After with 2.4 children and a dog. With Ian the family was already there. Each of Ian's children welcomed her, the grandchildren began calling her Granny Sue which was touching. With Ian there weren't the money worries that she had with Arnie when they were first starting off. Susan had no money worries, she didn't even have a mortgage thanks to Arnie and Betty; she was quite well off. It was more of a companionship with a bit of spice thrown in.

The guilt she had felt when she first started having a relationship passed. Arnie would want her to be happy. If the shoe was on the other foot she would have told Arnie to take happiness where he could.

LAST NOTE

As unexpected as it was, Susan embraced it.

There was talk of marriage, but it wasn't a necessity. Maybe when they got older they might talk more about it. For now having sleepovers a few nights a week was enough. And the holidays; always choosing somewhere neither of them had been before. Making fresh memories and not raking over old ones.

When Susan Cole was in receipt of £10 note HE75 229564 her life was in disarray. Grieving widow and borderline alcoholic; Susan could truly not see at that point that there was light at the end of the tunnel.

£10 HE75 229564 made little difference to Susan's life. It was just some change given to her when change was the one thing she couldn't do for herself at that point.

'Addiction is Giving up Everything for One Thing – Recovery is Giving up One Thing for Everything!'

Anon

8

Money for Nothing

Kenny Birmingham never touched £10 note HE75 229564. When Susan Cole had used their delivery service to dispose of her mother in laws old bed, she had doled out two £10 notes to the deliverymen, Kenny had not received £10 note HE75 229564, but what a story he had to tell.

Kenny Birmingham had been given the chance of such a bright future. Signed at a young age to one of the biggest football clubs in the North East; he had the world at his feet, and hands; he was a goalkeeper.

He had worked so hard at football, even after he took on a massive growth spurt and ended up the size of a house; he still honed his footballing skills and adapted his game from being a sprightly striker to a goliath in the goal posts. The hard work had paid off and he was on the verge of making it big.

Then one fateful night, his life turned upside down.

Out with another youngster from the club, a lad he had known almost all of his life; they had decided to go into the town and celebrate their inclusion in the clubs up and coming first team tour in America.

Both lads were young, only just turned 18, but as with the culture of the city; everyone knew who the youngsters were. They drank and drank and Kenny, unused to any extremes of anything got very drunk.

The upshot was that he woke the next morning in a strange hotel room with his friend Kyle and no recollection of how he got there the night before.

Kenny didn't like it. He could barely remember anything of the previous evening.

Vowing never to drink copious amounts of alcohol again, he was shocked when he was asked to go into the club and speak to the management.

What happened next changed Kenny's life forever. There had been a claim by a young 17 year old girl, that she had been invited to the hotel room with Kenny and Kyle. And they had raped her.

Kenny had no recollection of anything from that night, but he was pretty sure he would not have raped anyone. He'd had girlfriends in the past, but football was his life and even though he was still a young buck; sex wasn't everything to him.

The police had been brought in and the charges against Kenny and Kyle were being investigated. In the meantime both the players were suspended.

Kenny was physically sick. He didn't know what had happened. He couldn't even remember the girl! Allegedly they had met in the last bar they had been in, when last orders had been called Kenny and Kyle had said they would get a hotel room and carry on the party.

And that was when the rape had taken place.

As ill as it made Kenny feel, he really couldn't say that he hadn't raped the girl. Even when he said it in his head he didn't sound like he could say it with any conviction. All he had was hours and hours of blackness. Hours where he had bought drinks, walked along the Quayside, booked a hotel room and then made his way up the lift and into the room. How could he be sure that he hadn't done it?

The most overwhelming thing he felt though was shame.

Even if he hadn't done what the girl was accusing him of; he had still been suspended. It was something that he couldn't keep from his mam and dad. Just the thought of telling them brought another wave of sickness over him. But it was something he couldn't not do, they would wonder why he wasn't going to training, why he wasn't getting ready to go to America. Why he looked so ill.

Their disappointment was tangible.

Kenny's mam and dad had given up so much for Kenny. Money for the endless pairs of new football boots and trainers, the endless car rides to football training and matches. And the time they had invested.

For them though it had all paid off. Kenny had been on the verge of everything. Telling them was the worst thing that had ever happened to Kenny. Even though it was all just allegations; the suspension alone was enough. He had let them down, the look on their faces said it all.

Even his mam's comforting arms around him did

little to disperse the constant bile that was in his throat.

A week later Kenny was called back into the club. All the charges had been dropped. And so had Kenny.

There would be no contract, no trip to America.

Kenny Birmingham's football career was over.

For Kenny Birmingham his life at that point was somewhat over. Football had been his life, he hadn't done well at school because there had always been football. He didn't have any other skills because of football. He had no friends because of football.

The money he had saved whilst he earned a wage soon disappeared and he had no choice but to contact an uncle, the only person he knew who could maybe give him a job. Cap in hand; he used the excuse that he'd had a career ending injury and now needed a job.

Uncle Stan would have every reason to gloat. Kenny was the superstar of the family. But he hadn't; he just said that he would happily take Kenny on; an extra pair of safe hands would never go amiss. Kenny was never sure if that was a dig or not; what with Kenny being a goalkeeper; but if it was it was something that Kenny would never hold against him. Kenny was grateful for the job.

And that was that.

Football career over; Kenny joined his Uncle Stan and cousins and spent his days tooing and throwing bits of furniture. Avoiding football at all costs; it was just too painful.

Meeting Ange brought Kenny a different kind of happiness. It had virtually been love at first sight for both of them and the only thing he could compare the feeling with was saving all the penalties in a penalty shoot out!

And they were so happy. They were married and in no time they were parents to five little girls.

Kenny could never be sure if he was happy that there wasn't a football mad boy; the thought of running up and down the touchline supporting his boy and someone recognising him as that youngster that signed for that big club had always filled him with dread as each pregnancy progressed.

Uncle Stan had retired and Kenny took over the business. It had turned out to be quite a lucrative one and he bought a bigger house in a nice part of town and all was well with the Birmingham family.

The only fly in the ointment had been Kyle Logan. The other youngster accused on the ill-fated night in the hotel room.

Kenny and Kyle had never really been friends. They had come through the same ranks so spent a long time together. But calling them friends was a push. Whereas Kenny always had to work at his game; Kyle seemed to have lots of natural ability. And boy did he let everyone know about it. Never shy of blowing his own trumpet; Kenny tended to avoid him best he could.

If only he had avoided him one last time.

But Kyle Logan was someone that Kenny never kept

tabs on. Kenny had not seen sight of him since the day in the boardroom at the Club.

Fate always manages to throw a spanner in the works though and one day Kenny saw Kyle Logan's face splashed all over the back page of a discarded newspaper.

Whereas Kenny had walked away from football after his dismissal from the club; Kyle had stayed in the game and made his way through the lower leagues and had just signed for one of the biggest London clubs in the Premiership.

Kenny from then on in was obsessed with Kyle Logan.

The houses, the cars, the trophy girlfriends. Kyle's England call up. Transfer to a North West Premiership club. Kenny was obsessed with it all.

Ange thought he had sour grapes. Maybe for Kenny not playing football was a kick in the teeth; by Kyle Logan's lifestyle, never. He had everything and more he could possibly want.

Kyle Logan's career would be over in a short time. Kenny had a job for life and a wife who he knew was with him for himself and not because of what he had or who he played for. Kenny could remember even when he was a youngster and a girl chased after him; he was never sure if it was him or his name they were after. Ange was the real deal.

And as Kenny had predicted Kyle Logan retired and even though he appeared to be at every charitable event and reality TV show there was going; he was not what he was.

And life for Kyle Logan was about to get a whole lot worse.

Kim Shaw; the girl from the hotel room sold her story to one of the Sunday Tabloids.

Kenny had no idea why it happened when it did. Maybe there was a gagging order involved. But one Sunday there was the whole story for the world to see.

Kyle Logan had raped Kim Shaw as Kenny Birmingham lay sparked out on the sofa.

After almost 30 years; Kenny Birmingham now knew that he had not raped that girl in the hotel room.

Kenny cried for himself, and he cried for the girl; Kim Shaw.

The injustice of it all. Kyle Logan had lived the Life of Riley while Kenny had lost his career and Kim had lived her life as a victim.

It was over. If his mam and dad had ever had their doubts, there was none now to have.

Kyle Logan went to trial. Kenny sat through it all. Kyle escaped a custodial sentence but was placed on the Sex Offender's Record. For Kenny it was closure.

And Kenny found his passion for football again.

Having a successful business allowed him the luxury of being able to go off and gain his football coaching badges and before long he was coaching with one of the local lower league teams.

Life was good!

Life was made better when his youngest daughter; aptly named Keegan found her passion for football.

Kenny didn't think that he had ever discouraged any of his girls from playing or even following football; it just seemed to be an unspoken rule. But with her dad emersed in coaching football; Keegan saw her opportunity and took up the sport that she had played at school for years; all under the radar so her dad didn't find out.

Keegan Birmingham was a superstar.

Under her dad's guidance she went from strength to strength.

In no time at all Keegan was being picked up by big clubs; all wanting her to sign for them.

On her 16th birthday Keegan signed for the club she had been holding out for. Her dad's old club.

Ange and Kenny could not have been prouder as they stood with her in the boardroom where all those years earlier Kenny had watched his own football career slip away. Keegan Birmingham was so much more savvy than her dad. She was on the up and up and if she had learned anything from her dad; it was always to keep her eye on the ball.

For Kenny being back at the club was bitter sweet. It had changed almost beyond recognition. For a start there had not been much of a girls team in his day. There were girls but they weren't taken very seriously. Today the girls have access to the same facilities as their male counterparts. The leagues they played in were a mirror image of the male league and nowadays there was money to be made.

There were only a couple of faces that Kenny recognised and he went out of his way to speak to them. Everyone expressed their condolences; if condolences was the right word to use for the loss of a playing career. Nevertheless for Kenny it was another hurdle crossed, maybe he would even start to go and watch first team football again; as well as Keegan play.

And then the Covid Pandemic came as well as his first grandchild; a boy!

Life took on a different look for a while. The vans remained stationery; no one was moving anywhere; thankfully the Government introduced the furlough scheme or else Kenny had no idea how long he could have sustained the business.

Kenny stayed at home and Ange; still a care worker went out to work.

Two of the girls were still living at home; Jessie and Keegan. Ange caught covid; then Jessie but somehow even living in the same house with Ange and Jessie; it avoided Kenny and Keegan.

It was the strangest of times.

Kenny continued to coach Keegan; the football grounds wouldn't stay closed forever and if there was one thing they could do during the lockdowns; it was stay fit.

Restrictions started to lift.

Keegan was called back to training. There was going to be some sort of football; probably behind closed doors without the crowds; there would be no way of policing a 2 metre rule at a football ground; it was hard enough doing it in the supermarkets; it would just be impossible to enforce.

But there was hope of something.

Keegan came back from training asking if it was ok for her to give her dad's number to someone at the club. She didn't know why; just someone had asked for it.

For Kenny it was a puzzle.

He himself was back on the vans; there seemed to be so many people moving house; unexpectedly business was booming.

When the call came, Kenny went into shock.

The club asked if he could maybe do some coaching with the first team; especially the goalkeepers! It seemed a lot of the coaches had gone home at the beginning of lockdown and as yet they hadn't returned. Kenny did not need to be asked twice.

The removal business was thriving; but he had good staff and could easily oversee everything and be able to coach.

And that is what he did. Kenny Birmingham returned to the training ground and picked up his football career in the big league again.

When football went back to normal and many of the coaches returned; Kenny Birmingham was asked to stay on. There was a contract to be signed.

For Kenny it was a no brainer; but he had commitments elsewhere. He had Ange and the girls and he had a business. It wasn't as easy as it had been almost 40 years earlier.

But with a bit of thought and a lot of organising; Kenny Birmingham became Goalkeeping Coach at the club of his dreams. Ange stood next to him in the boardroom as he signed his contract. It would mean time away from home; but Ange and Kenny had been married long enough and been through enough that a few nights away wouldn't do them any harm.

Kenny Birmingham's life had turned somewhat of a full circle. This time he had the added bonus of watching his daughter's career flourish. And it truly was flourishing; Keegan Birmingham had just been picked for the under 18 Lionesses; it was probably more than her dad could ever have hoped for.

£10 note HE75 229564 may never have crossed Kenny Birmingham's path. But what a story he had to tell.

'Injustice Anywhere is a Threat to Justice Everywhere!'
Martin Luther King

9

A Pretty Penny

When Susan Cole doled out the £10 notes to the deliverymen; it was William who had received £10 note HE75 229564.

Of course, he would have; he was special.

William even had a special name; Billy the Kid.

But Billy wasn't a kid anymore. He had just turned 40. Apart from working with Kenny Birmingham on his delivery van every now and again; Billy had never had a job. His dad would jokingly say that Billy had been dropped on his head when he was a baby. Billy knew it was a joke, but still something must have happened because he certainly was nothing like his brother or sister.

Even his nieces and nephews seemed to be more independent than he was.

Though that wasn't strictly true anymore.

Billy now had a home of his own and he had a girlfriend, Tanya.

But back when Mrs Cole had handed over to Billy £10 note HE75 229564 he had been living at home with his mam and dad, helping Kenny out now and again and the extra money he had received as a tip went straight to his good friend Cha Cha.

Cha Cha worked in the Glass House in the City Centre. He had been there many times with his friends; sometimes after they had spent the night in their local pub, a few of them would jump into a taxi and head into town to watch girls dance and drink way into the night long after most pubs had closed.

Billy even sometimes went on his own.

Cha Cha had been one of the dancers at the Glass House. She always made time for Billy and would come and sit at the bar with him if she saw him. Cha Cha never asked if she could dance for him; Billy didn't mind that at all. Billy liked just to sit with her and look at her and take in the smell of her. She was the most beautiful girl he had ever seen.

But sometimes he could spend a whole night sitting at the bar and Cha Cha would be coming and going.

When he had got the little extra money in the shape of the tip off the nice lady with the bed; he had asked Cha Cha if she could dance for him. She had refused, but taking the money off Billy, including £10 note HE75 229564 she had led him to a little room where for the next ten or fifteen minutes they had sat next to each other and talked.

Billy felt very special indeed.

Spending a little bit time with Cha Cha whenever he could was something that Billy did for a very long time. Cha Cha never danced for him and even when his friends wooped with delight every time Cha Cha led him by the hand to the room; he had no idea what all the fuss was about.

Billy wasn't daft though. He had seen enough people on television and in films to know all about what boys and girls got up to. But even though he spent lots of time with Cha Cha, he had never wanted to lie on top of her and squash her. That really didn't seem like a very kind thing to do. He was big lad and Cha Cha was tiny girl.

When one night Cha Cha wasn't at the Green House. He sat at the bar for ages and ages thinking she was just busy. But after he sat about an hour he asked the barmaid if Cha Cha was working that night. Billy almost cried when she said that Cha Cha had left.

Billy was very upset for a very long time.

His mam suggested a holiday. She tried to explain to Billy that the holiday was something call 'recipe' and that he would be going with some other people like him and that she and his dad would not be going. It was only going to be for a week.

Billy did not like the idea of going at all. Billy did not like strangers. Everyone in Billy's life had been there for his whole life. Obviously not Cha Cha; but she had been different.

His mam had persisted though; even showed him where he would be going; Blackpool and Billy did admit that it looked very twinkly and maybe it would be ok and if he didn't like it he could just get someone to come and get him and take him home.

Billy loved his holiday; he did not want it to end.

In Blackpool he met Tanya who was on holiday away from her Grandma who looked after her.

Tanya smelt nice like Cha Cha. But it was only the smell that they had in common.

By the time his mam and dad greeted him a week later off the mini bus; Billy was in love. Not the type of love he had thought he had felt for Cha Cha. Cha Cha had been like the twinkly lights of Blackpool.

Tanya was more lovely. She knew a lot of stuff about a lot of stuff and she had been to Blackpool lots of times. She made Billy brave. When he said he couldn't do something; like riding on the rollercoaster; she told him he could and proved it by taking him on it and even though she held his hand all of the way around; she had been right and he could do it.

Billy's mam and dad saw such a change in their special boy. He and Tanya talked all of the time on the telephone and soon Tanya was coming to their house for her Sunday dinner on a regular basis. His mam and dad weren't getting any younger and for years they had worried what would happen to Billy when they stepped off the earth. Obviously, Billy had a brother and sister; but they had families of their own and even though Billy was no bother; he was no bother because his mam and dad did so much for him.

Billy's mam went to see his doctor. She told him of the difference in Billy since his holiday; since meeting Tanya really. The doctor said that Billy was more than capable of living and independent life; though he very much doubted that Billy would be able to have a physical relationship with his girlfriend; he had been on tablets for years to suppress any urges; but that had just been a precaution and the doctor said that the damage had been done a long time ago for him to have any type of sexual relationship.

The charity that took Billy on holiday could help Billy learn to have a more independent life; to cook and clean and to take care of himself and for the next few years he attended the centre as well as working the odd day here and there for Kenny.

And all the while he and Tanya got closer and closer.

There had been another couple of holidays; one to Alton Towers which Billy was not really keen on at all; but Tanya had been before and assured Billy that he would love it. Tanya was right as always and Billy had loved it.

Billy could not be sure if it was the rollercoasters that gave him butterflies in his tummy or the fact that whatever ride they went on; Tanya say very close to him and held his hand tightly.

A flat became available in the complex the charity supported. It was ear marked for Billy. He had shown how capable he was at living independently during the many times he had attended the centre. The only problem Billy had was leaving the security blanket that was his mam and dad.

The three of them went and looked at the flat. It was small; really not much bigger than Billy's bedroom at home, in Billy's eyes anyway. But it had a small kitchen and a bathroom and it had a nice view across the local park.

Billy's mam and dad could see by how agitated Billy was that he was torn. As much as it pained them; they knew that it was going to take them to encourage him to take the flat on. Listing all of the benefits; that he could have his X Box in the living room instead of in his bedroom; that they could put his big television on the wall instead of on a unit.

Billy was still unsure.

Then by some sort of miracle Tanya was offered a flat in the same complex. From what Billy's mam and dad could make out; Tanya had always been a lot more independent; her Grandma was quite old so Tanya had done more caring for her than her Grandma had for Tanya; in recent years anyway.

But now her Grandma needed extra support and Tanya had requested that she too go to the complex where Billy would be going.

This information entirely changed the playing field. Billy could not get packed up quickly enough.

And so it was; Billy moved out of his mam and dad's home and all the comfort, security and support that was there for him and into his own little flat.

Billy's mam and dad had no misgivings. Billy needed it. They were both aging and wouldn't be around forever and to be honest; they needed the rest. For almost 40 years; Billy had been their life. Even having their younger children; they always had an eye on Billy.

As it happened; Billy moved into his flat just as the whole country went into Lockdown.

It was thought that they would bring Billy home; but he wouldn't hear of it. The complex became a small independent island. No one in and no one out; unless for essentials. Billy's mam and dad's contact became Zoom calls or a visit to the gate where they could talk to Billy and check that he was doing ok.

He was. He managed to do online shops; there were carers on hand for anything he needed and he saw lots of Tanya; who by all accounts was missing her Grandma more than she could ever know and was very sad in parts.

Billy caught Covid; how no one knew because the residents had been very cosseted. But the majority of the residents and staff caught it and for Billy's mam and dad it was a very scary time. All they had were daily updates on how Billy was doing; he was so poorly he couldn't even summon up the strength to talk to them on the telephone.

The doctor thought about having Billy admitted into hospital; he wasn't improving. Tanya became their lifeline; she herself had caught Covid too; but she had recovered quickly and now spent her days helping look after Billy. She would Facetime Billy's mam and dad so they could see for themselves how Billy was. It had been a blessing and a curse. Sometimes ignorance is bliss and for Billy's mam and dad; seeing how very poorly Billy was caused them no end of worry.

It was so difficult for them not being able to see him and take care of him; up until quite recently they had cared for Billy every day of his life.

Just as the doctor thought about the hospital admission; Billy rallied a bit. Nothing major; just a slight improvement; but it was enough for the doctor to decide that it would be more detrimental to his condition to move him.

Billy began to recover. Very slowly.

But recover he did and although the doctor felt that from then on in Billy would always have a weak chest; it was far better than the alternative. The number of people lost to the alien virus grew every day.

They all made it through the Lockdowns.

It was thought Billy had something they called 'Long Covid', he got tired very quickly, caught coughs and colds off anyone that sneezed within a 5 mile radius of him and struggled walking long distances or up flights of stairs.

The worst thing for Billy was that when Kenny Birmingham rang him to go back and work on the delivery vans; Billy had to say no. There was no way he could carry a sofa nowadays.

But he had Tanya and she helped fill his days.

They would travel on buses to different places; Billy loved it best when they went to the coast and ate fish and chips. It reminded him of when he had first met Tanya in Blackpool.

Every Sunday Billy's dad would collect Billy and Tanya from the complex and they would go and have Sunday Lunch with the family and on the way back visit Tanya's Grandma in her care home. It was Billy and Tanya's favourite day of the week.

Billy adored Tanya and Tanya adored Billy.

It was no surprise to the families when Billy and Tanya said they wanted to marry.

There was no reason not to.

Tanya had spoken to Billy's mam. Tanya said her Grandma was too old and too poorly to talk to it about and she did not want to talk to the carers. Tanya told Billy's mam that although she loved Billy with all of her heart; she did not think that she was capable of anything beyond kissing Billy. The physical part of a relationship; which Tanya knew all about was not something she could do. With assurances that Billy would not expect or want anything beyond the kissing; there was no reason in Tanya's mind why her and Billy could not be married.

It was a marriage of companionship.

And so, Billy and Tanya married.

It was the loveliest of days. Tanya's Grandma had even gone; it must have been such a relief for her knowing that not only did Tanya have a husband but also all of the support and love from Billy's family too. A week after the wedding Tanya's Grandma slipped away in her sleep.

Today Billy and Tanya are packing up their little flat.

They are staying on the complex but as the first married couple they have had to wait sometime until a flat big enough for them both was available.

They had been given it a week earlier, but Tanya wanted it decorated and some new carpets; it would be their forever home.

More good news for Billy and Tanya was for the first time in three years; they were going on holiday. Blackpool; their place. Tanya said there was a new rollercoaster for them to ride. Billy wasn't sure, but he would do it. Tanya would sit close to him and hold his hand…

£10 note HE75 229564 did not have much bearing on Billy's life. He gave it away cheaply to a girl that worked in a club. It may have been worth more to her than it had to him. But then again if Billy hadn't given it to Cha Cha who he thought of as a friend, her subsequent disappearance from his life; his sadness and his mam recognising his sadness and making him go on the holiday to Blackpool he would never had met Tanya; the only girl he ever wanted to sit close to him and hold his hand!

'In Every Single Thing You Do, You Are Choosing a Direction. Your Life is a Product of Choices!'

Dr Kathleen Hall

10

Fool's Gold

Lindsey Kinghorn was one of the recipients of £10 note HE75 229564.

That had been a long time ago. A time when Lindsey was more her alto ego than she was herself.

Lindsey was at university at the time. Living in digs it was not only the need for a bit extra money but a place where she could be; living in strange city with only the people she met at university who she could call friends.

On reflection; Lindsey could probably have got a job anywhere, bar jobs were ten a penny for students or she could have got a job in a shop. She was presentable and spoke well having been brought up in the South. But someone had told her about The Glass House; it played to her strengths and her parents would hate it.

And so there was Cha Cha! The girl who gyrated way into the night when she should have been studying or sleeping. But even after only working there one night; Lindsey loved it. She loved the power it gave her; the lust she saw in men's eyes was intoxicating; sadly not as intoxicating as the little pills she took to keep her awake and alert long enough for her to make it through her days at university and her nights at The Glass House.

'Fool's Gold' they had called the pills. Lindsey had been a fool for ever taking them; but hindsight is a wonderful thing and maybe if she hadn't taken them she may not have ended up living the life she was now.

It had been a hard lesson to learn though.

At first she had managed fine; she danced a few nights a week and the rest of the week she would be tucked up in bed at a reasonable hour with the knowledge that whatever assignment she had needed to do was complete. A private education certainly was a bonus when it came to being disciplined with regard to her coursework.

Working at the Glass House gave Lindsey an excuse not to go home at weekends. Not that her mum and dad knew what type of establishment their daughter worked in; it wasn't the type of thing one tells your parents Lindsey said to herself as she told them that she was working in a club and that would mean getting home for weekends would be difficult.

To Lindsey, her parents were tuppence halfpenny snobs. Something she could see more and more the greater distance she put between them. Lindsey was their trophy daughter. The little girl that had always been seen and not heard. The little girl who had excelled at everything she put her mind to and she knew that they were very proud of her, but still.

Lindsey had never been anywhere with her mum just on her own. If there was to be an outing to buy clothes or some new ballet or tap shoes; then Lindsey's Grandma would be there too. Lindsey didn't mind her Grandma being there; she had helped bring Lindsey up when her mum and dad were busy with work or their hectic social life. But still! Was it normal for a mum to need a buffer between herself and her daughter?

But Lindsey had wanted for nothing. The dance classes had stood her well for working at The Glass House; not that she ever did any of the dances she had been taught since she was a tot, but still, she knew how to move and she knew by the looks on the punters faces; that could be mesmerising.

Lindsey loved working at The Glass House. The girls that worked there were all amazing. They all had a story as to why they were there; there were even a couple of girls there that went to the same university as Lindsey or Cha Cha as she was known in the club.

Linda Glass owned The Glass House. Cha Cha was in total awe of her. She had started up The Glass House from scratch; a former stripper, she had worked the dubious club circuit in the North East. What she didn't know about stripping could be written on the back of a postage stamp. She was a legend.

And Cha Cha loved the punters. It had been one of them that had given her £10 note HE75 229564. Billy had paid for Cha Cha to give him a dance in one of the little rooms at the back of the club. Billy had paid Cha Cha lots of times for dances. But Cha Cha never danced. She didn't even like taking the money off him; but he would insist and they would make their way to into one of the little rooms. Then for the next 10 minutes or so they would just sit next to each other and talk.

It was a refreshing change for Cha Cha. Most of the punters would be grabbing at her and asking if she did any extras.

Cha Cha never did any extras though she did suspect some of the girls did. She loved the dancing part of her job, but going beyond that was not her bag. Even when she had been at her most desperate; when the little pills had done their worst on her she didn't succumb to an extra tenna here and there.

Poor Billy didn't even ask for a dance. He told her not long after he started coming to The Glass House that he was special. To be honest to look at him Cha Cha couldn't really tell that he had any issues; he looked just like the rest of the group of friends that he had come in with. But once the conversation had been struck up between them, it became apparent.

Billy said that he had been dropped on his head as a baby, but had no lumps or bumps so thought that his dad was fibbing. Cha Cha thought that there had more than likely been a complication at his birth; a friend of hers back home had an older sister who Billy reminded her of; Effie had been starved of oxygen. Maybe that was what had happened to Billy too.

But he was one of Cha Cha's regulars and she always made sure she made time for him; even if he didn't have the money for Cha Cha to take him into the little room. They would sit together at the bar and when Cha Cha went off to work; Billy would wait patiently for her to come back.

The Glass House was an education all in itself. Cha Cha probably learned more there than she did at university. The punters came in all shapes and sizes. Some thought they were Cock of the North; other's timid and shy like they had never seen a girl up close and personal before. The married ones who fancied their chances; the stags that were on their last hurrah and then there were the lonely ones; the ones that had the money to spend because they had no one to go home to.

Cha Cha learned to read them all the minute they arrived. With time she even learned to suss out the ones that would be wanting some additional and would give them a wide berth. There was always security on hand, but it wasn't worth the aggravation.

By the time Cha Cha was in her final year at university; she was working most nights in The Glass House. Her course work was beginning to suffer and when her regular taxi driver offered to give her something to pep her up; she took it.

Fool's Gold.

Foolish Cha Cha!

Pretty soon, Cha Cha was handing over money for the Fool's Gold nearly every night she worked. She would jump in the taxi with Mark the driver and he would hand over a little packet to her and she would hand him some of the money she had earned in return. If she took the little pills on the journey home then by the time she got into her house; scrubbed off Cha Cha, then she could work long into the night on university work and only need a few hours' sleep.

The Fool's Gold was addictive though. Soon one pill became two to get the same outcome; then three and then she wasn't sure how many she was taking. All she knew was that she couldn't function without them.

They gave her nightmares when she did sleep, she had no appetite and the only way she could get through a night in The Glass House was because she knew that Mark would be outside in the taxi waiting for her with her little bag of pills.

Despite everything she made it through her final year. She was skin and bone; jittery and a shadow of Lindsey who had started worked at The Glass House a couple of years earlier. Going home the previous Christmas had been an ordeal; she feigned flu for the state of her. Her mum and dad seemed to buy that and for once she wasn't paraded in front of their friends at the Christmas Eve Soiree. Not able to cope being there another minute; she made excuses and left early on Boxing Day morning.

The state of their daughter must have sent some alarm bells ringing. Money was deposited into her bank account and there was a daily phone call from one of them. Of course Cha Cha shook it all off; it had just been flu. Did they know how cold the North East was in the summer never mind winter. Her biggest fear was they would just turn up. They didn't and once Cha Cha was back working and taxiing home with Mark she coped.

Well, she thought she did.

When one night she went to jump in the taxi only to find that it wasn't Mark; Cha Cha thought she would die.

She almost did.

If Linda Glass hadn't had some sort of second sight; Cha Cha thought she may have well died. There had only been her living at the digs; all the rest of her fellow students had moved out. Cha Cha only hadn't because she was so out of it all of the time and never had enough energy to pack up her belongings and find somewhere else to live.

It had been Linda Glass that had found a very broken Cha Cha wrapped up in a duvet in a living room armchair.

Linda Glass saved Cha Cha's life; there would have been no reason for anyone to go to Cha Cha's house. No friends close enough to notice Cha Cha's absence. No boyfriend, maybe her parents may have raised the alarm at some point. But Cha Cha had been living an erratic lifestyle so her parents would have presumed that she was just busy and maybe left it a good week before they became concerned.

Mrs Glass had collected all Cha Cha's belongings; bundled the comatose girl into the back of her car and then secured the house. Cha Cha wouldn't be going back there.

Instinct told her that as poorly as Cha Cha seemed to be; she had caught her in enough time for her not to need to go into hospital. Mrs Glass had spent enough time to know how hard Cha Cha had worked for her degree. A degree that would enable her to teach; a record for drug taking would be doing her no favours; even if it was just on a medical report.

So Linda Glass took Cha Cha to her own home in a tiny village a few miles out of Newcastle.

She had carried the sleeping girl into her spare bedroom. She had stripped her of her scruffy clothes; washed her best she could and then bundled her into bed. And then she waited.

A million times she thought to ring for an ambulance or at the very least a doctor; but something told her not to. That Cha Cha would wake up and then they would deal with whatever it was that Cha Cha had been taking!

It was over 24 hours before Cha Cha opened her eyes. By then Mrs Glass had took her manager into her confidence. She had to. She was missing from The Glass House and that had never happened before. Jordan had come to the house as soon as he could and as they looked down on the bed at the sleeping bundle; the bundle began to move and Cha Cha opened her eyes and looked at them both in surprise, before closing them again and heading back off into another deep sleep.

That had been the beginning though. Lindsey could remember that moment that she had woken up from the nightmare. She had stared up at the face of her bosses and knew that she had a chance. When she went back to sleep the nightmares were there again; but somehow she knew that she was no longer in them alone. Mrs Glass was at the side of her bed and she knew that somehow she wouldn't leave her.

It ended up being a very slow recovery.

Each day Lindsey felt a little better. The whole cold turkey thing had been the worst, but she had survived it and after that it was just a case of resting and getting some of her strength back.

Linda was her guardian angel. Her home became Lindsey's and over the following weeks and months they built up a relationship which was no longer Boss and Dancer.

Cha Cha was gone and she wouldn't be coming back. Lindsey couldn't risk lapsing into old ways.

Gradually Lindsey began to emerge. There was no fake tan or false eye lashes. Her skin, which had been covered in spots began to clear. She was such a better version of herself.

Linda Glass said her home was Lindsey's for as long as she needed it, Lindsey was so grateful. She would read or listen to music or one of the DVD's in Mrs Glass's mammoth library. It was Lindsey's own form of rehab and it was working.

Her friendship with Linda Glass was salve for her wounds. Her heart was a different story.

Jordan Kinghorn.

Lindsey had always liked him when she had been Cha Cha. The girls all said that he was their bit of eye candy.

And he was. Tall dark and handsome; the girls actually swooned at him. But to all accounts he had a very chequered past, including a wife and child somewhere.

But every day he had driven over to his boss's house to help care for Cha Cha. Like Mrs Glass; Lindsey thought he felt some sort of responsibility. Neither of them did. It had been all her own doing how she had got into the mess she was. Lindsey was just grateful that they had taken such good care of her.

Even when Lindsey was somewhat back on her feet; Jordan came over every day.

At first Lindsey was shy and very embarrassed about what had happened. With Mrs Glass working back at The Glass House and never rising from her bed until lunch time; Lindsey and Jordan spent mornings together. Sometimes they would just sit and drink coffee; other times they would walk and talk.

Jordan Kinghorn certainly did have a chequered past. And a wife and a son. The latter still being part of Jordan's life, the former less so but as a friend. And Jordan had been around the block many times. Lindsey should have been running for the hills.

It was a warts and all type of friendship. There was nothing off limits and despite everything Lindsey found herself falling in love. That was all she needed after what she had just put herself through.

Lindsey thought it was maybe loneliness that made her fixate on Jordan. Apart from him and Mrs Glass and Mrs's Glass mam; she saw no one. Anything she wanted she bought on-line; but aside from the basics; there was nothing she needed.

It had taken weeks and weeks; but Lindsey was beginning to feel more like her old self; her appetite was returning with vengeance mainly thanks to her walks and all the fresh air she took in. And she slept soundly. There were no nightmares; no monsters with human heads chasing her night after night after night. Now if she had a dream it was about something naughty with Jordan that would make her cheeks flush the next time she saw him.

Maybe she just needed to have sex!

Lindsey O'Brien's Do-it-Yourself Rehabilitation was complete. Looking in the mirror in Mrs Glass's bathroom, if she said so herself, she looked a picture of health. Her hair was in need of a good cut; the hair extensions had done some damage. But even though it was all sorts of lengths; it shone. Her skin was clear and all the sores and abrasions in and around her mouth were gone.

She was still a bit on the skinny side; but she had never been very big. Her boobs looked a bit like empty crisp packets; but if they didn't fill back out there was always chicken fillets or at worst a boob job.

Lindsey looked about 18 years old. All traces of Cha Cha had gone!

She had so much to be thankful of Mrs Glass for. Saving her; not taking her to hospital where her drug addiction would be on her medical history. For not calling her mum and dad. For allowing Jordan to help. For letting Lindsey live with her until she healed. The list was endless.

There was a great big world in front of Lindsey. She just needed to decide what it was she wanted to do! And she was ready to make that decision.

Somehow in all the Cha Cha madness, Lindsey had managed to get herself a good degree.

Her mum and dad were very proud; they told her every time she called them. They had bought the story that Lindsey had become somewhat exhausted after university and was staying with a friend at her country retreat. They didn't just buy it; Lindsey knew without a shadow of a doubt that they would be telling all their friends how Lindsey was staying at some country retreat in Northumberland. They hadn't mentioned Graduation. It had come and gone and there was no photograph of Lindsey in her Cap and Gown for them to show off on Facebook.

But they had never asked why she hadn't attended Graduation. They hadn't mentioned her going home or suggested that they come up North. They had not seen sight of each other for over 6 months; it didn't seem to faze either party.

Lindsey's degree that nearly killed her was also her greatest asset. It gave her opportunity; she refused to waste it.

With a little bit research on the internet; a few emails and she had applied to do her teacher training.

If Mrs Glass had any reservations about Lindsey returning to Newcastle and all its trappings there for Lindsey; she didn't voice them. She said that Lindsey was to stay there at the cottage with her until she had finished the course.

Mrs Glass could see that the broken girl from months earlier was now a woman with a fire in her belly and a heartful of love not only for herself, but for The Glass House Deputy Manager; Jordan Kinghorn. Even if they didn't know it themselves; Linda Glass had seen it materialise before her very eyes. Jordan may have once had a reputation for wandering hands; now all Mrs Glass saw that he was a safe pair of hands for Lindsey.

So Lindsey went back to Newcastle and back to University. This time University had her full focus; she enjoyed lectures, adored her placements and took all her assignments in her stride. There were no demons in the city for her.

Lindsey made new friends; even went on a few dates. But her friendship with Jordan continued to flourish. They would meet for lunch, or if work permitted it; he would drive her back to the cottage. For Lindsey, Jordan was the real deal. If she could have dug deep and summoned up her inner Cha Cha she would have made a move on him. But she was Lindsey and all she could do was accept the friendship; hope that he felt the same way and let it develop.

Almost to the day that Lindsey nearly died as Cha Cha; Jordan kissed Lindsey O'Brien. It was the real deal for both of them.

LAST NOTE

They married at Gretna Green six weeks later. Lindsey O'Brien to Cha Cha to Lindsey O'Brien to Mrs Lindsey Kinghorn in just over a year.

Mrs Glass was a witness; she could not have been more pleased or prouder if she had married herself. Something she never planned on doing again but turning up with The Glass House Accountant to the wedding to be the second witness; had been a bit of a shock. Neither Jordan or Lindsey realised that when Mrs Glass said that she would be bringing her 'gentleman friend' with her to the wedding that it would be the stern faced accountant that came to The Glass House on a regular basis. Still waters run deep!

Mr and Mrs Jordan Kinghorn could not have been happier.

They had both travelled a long and arduous road to find each other. More remarkable was the fact that Lindsey had seen Jordan nearly every day when she worked at The Glass House when she was Cha Cha and he had not seen her.

It wasn't until she was stripped back of the hair extensions; fake eyelashes and nails; make-up and skimpy outfits did he really see Cha Cha for who she was and fell in love with her.

For both of them their past was their past and it was the present that counted.

Lindsey had no qualms about him working in The Glass House; his philandering ways had lost him his first marriage; Lindsey knew without a shadow of a doubt that he would not let that happen again. The future was bright for them both.

Jordan's little boy Elliott became a regular visitor at Lindsey and Jordan's home. A one they had chosen together in a village between Newcastle and Mrs Glass's cottage in the hamlet. Elliott and Lindsey got on straight away; he would mimic Lindsey's posh southern accent and she would put on a heavy Geordie twang back at him. They all laughed when Lindsey shouted 'Howay man Elliott Ya Tea's Redy!'

Lindsey got a teaching post in a primary school a few miles from their new home. She loved it. She was teaching 5/6 year olds; any trepidation as to whether or not teaching was for her was well and truly put to bed. Duck to water.

Jordan went south with Lindsey and met her mum and dad. They had been shocked when she had called to say that she was married; Lindsey did feel bad, only daughter, only child and all that and when after the initial phone call to say they were married her mum called her back and asked if she could bring Jordan home with her and that they would have a small celebration, Lindsey felt she had no choice but to say yes.

Obviously, the small celebration had nothing small about it.

Memories of her childhood and being brought down from her bedrooms for such occasions in the past flooded her mind. She was a trophy daughter. But she endured it, everyone made such a fuss of her and Jordan.

They ended up staying a week. They made it their honeymoon.

But for Lindsey the Motorway sign for the A1 had never been so welcoming. She may have had a dodgy accent, but Lindsey was a Geordie!

Married life suited Lindsey and Jordan. Elliott stayed some weekends and in the holidays. They had a good social life; often with Linda; which both Lindsey and Jordan had given in and started calling her; and Linda's 'gentleman friend' Dave, who was nowhere near as stern as his face led him to be.

Nico Kinghorn arrived weighing 7lb 7ozs which Lindsey thought was big for her tiny frame. It then made sense why she had been the size of a house. He was perfect in every way. For days and days Lindsey and Jordan would just sit and look at him.

He was their miracle. Lindsey's body never really went back into its normal monthly rhythm; there was no indication as to whether she could even have a baby. They had scrapped precautions and let fate take its course. Lindsey had been four months pregnant before she had even detected that there was a baby there.

So Nico was special to them; there may never be another. But they had Elliott and they had Nico and for them that would be enough.

Covid hit, the country went into Lockdown and The Glass House closed.

Lindsey, Jordan and Nico lived in their little bubble together for months. Elliott was a little face on the screen and Mrs Glass and Dave; who happened to be staying at the cottage when Lockdown happened both caught Covid 19.

Dave recovered quickly, but Mrs Glass had a weak chest, which she told Lindsey was due to the fact that she had stripped for years and years in cold workingmen's clubs and often had blue tits; took a very long time to get back to normality.

There was no indication as to when The Glass House would reopen. Dave; the savvy stern accountant made sure that every scheme the Government launched was applied for and for Mrs Glass and Jordon there was hope that once things got back to normal, there would still be a business to run.

Lindsey was asked to help out at the school. Her maternity leave was almost over and the thought of seeing her class every day thanks to Zoom calls filled her heart with joy. It was a very surreal experience.

The children would be sitting doing lessons in their pyjamas; often with interruptions from mams, dads, brothers and sisters, cats and dogs. But at least they were all seeing each other and knew that the Lockdown malarkey wasn't just happening to them.

It was the sweetest thing when the children all shouted hello to each other through the screen.

Restrictions lifted. The Glass House remained closed but Lindsey could go back into school and teach the children face to face.

It was a bit of a culture shock for teachers and

children alike. At first they were all boisterous and unruly; it had been so long since they had all been together. The boisterous ones she could cope with, it was the quiet ones she was struggling with; most of them were only 5 years old and because they had been home for so long; they seemed to have regressed to being insular and in some cases, more babyfied.

Every day there seemed to be one of them poorly and Lindsey would have to arrange for them to be sent home; most of them would just have a cold, but there was no way the whole class and beyond could risk the chance that it may be Covid.

Nico was two years old when his daddy went back to work. It had taken that long for restrictions to be lifted enough for the gentleman's club to be open its doors. Even then there were rules in place, but Mrs Glass and Jordon knew that once the doors opened the punters would return. They would look at other income revenues within the Club to make money if need be.

A creche not far from Lindsey's school had been found for Nico. Any fears that Lindsey and Jordon had about leaving their son in someone else's care was soon allayed. Nico loved it and settled in so well that on occasion he would cry when Lindsey picked him up for home and he had to leave his little playmates.

For Lindsey Kinghorn having £10 note HE75 229564 was of little odds for her. She had it in her possession such a short time. It was handed over to her supplier within hours in exchange for the little pills that almost killed her.

Lindsey had been lucky. She had lived to tell the tale.

Cha Cha was part of her makeup. She had learned so much about life from Cha Cha. Inadvertently her life today would not be as it was without her. She thought herself to be a better judge of character; had more empathy and an understanding of addictions. Maybe one day she would put all of her skills to use and become a counsellor or something.

But for now she was happy with her lot. She had a new class; this time an older year group which unexpectedly brought her face to face with her past.

Parents evening! It was one of Lindsey's favourite nights of the year. She loved meeting her children's parents. It was a chance to air any concerns she had about the children; there were so many since they had returned to school. So many of her class's mams and dads seemed to have split up; she even had a couple of children that were living with other relatives. Lockdown had a lot to answer for.

Lindsey liked to think that she could be approached by parents at any point so always went out of her way to forge a relationship with them on parents evening. She herself would always want to know if Elliott's or if sometime in the future Nico was not doing well at school.

She had no such concerns with India Dickens. She was a sweet girl who worked hard at her class work and mixed well with her classmates. There would be no reason for Lindsey to raise the alarm to India's mam and dad.

Lindsey spotted him whilst he and his wife were in the queue. He was facing sideways to her but she would have recognised his profile anywhere.

It was Mark, her taxi driver!

Lindsey was unsure what to do. He clearly would not know her as Mrs Kinghorn or Miss Kinghorn as she was known at school.

She had no idea who his child was; his surname was something she never knew. She only ever knew him as Mark.

Mark who had been kind to her when he took her home from The Glass House. Mark who had only suggested something to help her get through her University assignment when she left The Glass House dead on her feet after dancing all night.

Mark who had warned her that he had no idea what was in the pills. All he knew was that they were called 'Fool's Gold' and they were some type of upper.

Mark who had carried on selling her pills way beyond the assignment and when it would have become apparent that she was becoming addicted on them.

Mark who left her high and dry one night. The night that she almost died. The night that was the beginning of the end of 'Fool's Gold' and all the consequences that held in store.

Mark!!

Lindsey was unsure how she felt about him. But he was in the queue to see her and she had little choice but to sit and face him and see what happened from there.

Mark and his wife sat on the chairs opposite Lindsey. Mark looked directly at her and smiled. He clearly did not recognise her.

His wife was smiling too. 'We are India Dickens mam and dad!'

Lindsey smiled at them both and started to talk about how well India was doing. As she spoke she watched the colour drain out of Mark Dickens face. He may not have recognised her face when he sat down in front of her. But the voice he did know. Her clipped Southern tone.

And then it was over.

Mark Dickens said nothing beyond 'thank you!.

Mark Dickens, Dickens was his surname. What were the chances of his daughter being in her class.

It beggared belief!

An hour or so later Parents Evening was over for that term and Lindsey was making her way out to her car.

Mark Dickens and his wife were standing at the entrance, obviously waiting for Lindsey.

'Cha Cha????'

For the next half an hour Lindsey, Mark and his wife Anna talked. Lindsey had been right he hadn't recognised her; it had been the voice that gave her away, once her heard that he saw something in Lindsey he recognised. To be fair to Mark; he had never seen

Lindsey in daylight; the best it had ever been had been as dawn was breaking.

He apologised for everything. Filled Lindsey in on the reason why he hadn't picked her up that last night and everything that happened after that. Lindsey told him what she could remember happening to her after that.

Mark told her he had gone to The Glass House looking for her when he could. How he had spoken to the owner when she decided she would give him the time of day. Somewhere in a distant memory Lindsey thought that she could remember Mrs Glass telling her the taxi driver had been to see her. But at the time it had all just been blah blah blah and she hadn't comprehended what had been said.

The conversation wasn't awkward. Mark could not have been more sorry; he didn't know what he had given her, just that he should have stopped it when she was buying more and more. Lindsey told him how she was still connected to The Glass House. That she still popped in on occasions either to see her husband Jordan or Mrs Glass. And no she was never tempted to have a dance!

Cha Cha was in her past. Mark had put Mark the taxi driver in the past. Both had learned and moved on.

New towns, new jobs, new lives.

If Mark and Anna had thought that India would suffer because of what Mark had done to Lindsey, they were mistaken. Lindsey wasn't like that and before they parted ways she made it very clear to India Dickens parents.

Miss Kinghorn got into her car and drove off in the direction of her house. Back to her home where Jordon was waiting for her with Nico. £10 note HE75 229564 didn't change her life, that had been given to Cha Cha.

Cha Cha, her alto ego who had changed her life. Better in the end. Much, much better in the end….

'A Fool May Have His Coat Embroidered With Gold, But It Is A Fool's Coat Still!'

Antoine Rivarol

11

In for a Penny in for a Pound

Mark Dickens remembered very well the night that he had sat in front of his daughter's primary school teacher and was confronted with his past.

He was so shocked and relieved that he had not heard a word that Miss Kinghorn had said about India and her achievements. It wasn't until later that Anna had told him that India was doing amazing.

Mark Dickens had been in possession of £10 note HE75 229564.

On reflection it had seemed like a lifetime ago. Mark had been a taxi driver at the time but had a side hustle selling some dubious merchandise. For the life of him he had no idea how he had even got into the game. A chance conversation here and there and the next thing he was offered the chance to make quite a lot of money.

The taxi and the drugs was something that Mark Dickens could never have imagined himself doing. When it was decided that he wasn't going to be the next Alan Shearer he had secured himself a position as an apprentice electrician and thought that was where his future lay. But the company went bust and he lost his job not long after qualifying.

With little experience as an electrician; there was no work.

The only thing that he could think he could do was use his meagre savings to buy a car and get himself his Hackney badge.

But taxi driving had been soul destroying. There was so much waiting around time; even with his regular customers, he would find himself sitting idling in his taxi more than he would on the road.

If he worked long enough hours it paid its way though. Until Anna and the baby.

Anna had been a fare that Mark had cheekily given his mobile number to. They had met up and got out a few times and after they had been together 3 months or so Anna discovered that she was 2 months pregnant. At the time Mark was devastated; as well as him and Anna got on, it was all a bit too soon. But there was no way he would abandon her after she said adamantly that she would not be getting rid of the baby.

Mark moved in and together they made the best of a bad job. Money was tight and no matter how many hours he worked; they were always skint.

They took out a payday loan; when that got too much they took out another to pay for the first; it was relentless. By the time Anna started her maternity leave Mark felt like he was living in a hamster wheel. It was relentless.

The only bright light in his life was the baby girl that Anna was having. No matter how tired or how stressed he was; he had no resentment towards the baby. Or Anna for that matter. They were getting on well enough; she couldn't have felt any better about the situation than Mark. Working at the local leisure centre; she had been about to embark on a course to become a personal trainer when she fell wrong. That wouldn't be happening anytime soon. They muddled along together making the best of a bad job.

One of Mark's regulars in his taxi was a bloke called Jason Lee. Mark hadn't known him before he became a regular but he had heard of him. Local lad made good was how everyone described him; but there was an edge about him and without ever having met him; Mark knew that Jason Lee had his finger in some very saucy pies.

Jason Lee ran one of the city centres best clubs. When he lost his driving licence he taxied from the club every night to his home on the outskirts of town. When one night it had been Mark taking him home and they had struck up conversation he had taken Mark's number and asked if he would mind collecting him at the end of each night.

Mark was over the moon. It was a good fare and Jason Lee tipped well. And they got on well enough. Jason Lee was always interested in Mark and his life. And Mark found himself liking Jason Lee; fierce reputation or not. Jason Lee was a self-made man, came from nothing and Mark was impressed with what he had now; even if he had got it by hook and by crook.

LAST NOTE

The Lodge where Jason Lee lived looked nothing like a Lodge that Mark had ever seen; it was like a castle complete with fortress like gates. It was immense; the flat that he shared with Anna and the soon to arrive baby could literally fit into one of the bedrooms.

Knowing all about Mark's plight with regard to money, Mark wasn't surprised when on one of the journey's home, Jason suggested Mark do some work for him. Mark didn't need to be explained to what the work would entail. In regard to drugs Mark was as green as the grass; it had been something he had never been in to. When he thought that he was going to be the next Alan Shearer he had avoided all of the temptations in his youth; even when he was a young apprentice drugs had been something other people did; it just wasn't him.

Mark opened his mouth to say no but found himself saying yes. He just wanted everything for Anna and the baby. Jason Lee said it was lucrative; even if he did it until Anna went back to work that would be enough.

And so Mark Dickens started his second apprenticeship; this time he was being taught off the Grand Master; Jason Lee.

Jason Lee had said that there was money to be made and he wasn't wrong. In no time at all Mark had managed to get rid of the Pay Day loans; give Anna money and start his own little rainy day fund. It was all a bit too easy.

Mark hated it.

Mark loved the money though!

Anna gave birth to India and Mark's goal posts changed again. He had no idea that he would feel such huge emotions for a tiny baby. And for Anna too; the woman who had given him his daughter. Any thought that he would be giving up the side hustle when the baby arrived were well and truly out of the window. He wanted to give India the world.

The taxi driving and the drug dealing worked hand in hand. All a little bit too easy.

Punters would book a taxi; they would do the deal on the journey and then the drug money would be paid when they paid their fare. The drugs would be handed over as change; easy.

And the people that bought off Mark would constantly surprise him.

Obviously there were the likely lot; the ones that looked like they needed them. But there were others. Doctors, solicitors, teachers, students; Mark even had a few pensioners who weren't adverse to what they like to call 'treating themselves'

And all the time Mark had his eye in the rear view mirror; the thought of being arrested made him sick to his stomach; the only saving grace he had was that he never carried too much; at a push he could get away with saying they were for his own personal consumption.

But still!

Jason Lee had been pleased with his protégé. Every night Mark would order more and more drugs and hand over the money to Jason Lee; somewhere in a batch of money £10 note HE75 229564 passed to him. But it was just one of hundreds and hundreds of notes he handed over. Mark often wondered how much money actually went through the electric gates and into the Lodge.

It would be mouth-watering!

Mark didn't like to think of himself as a drug dealer; it didn't sit well. When he did any dealings he took on that funny third person scenario so it was like it was someone else doing all the dodgy dealings and he was just looking on; it was the only way he would be able to sleep in his bed. He could not have a conscious.

But Cha Cha gave him a conscious.

She was a regular who he picked up in the early hours of the morning from The Glass House; the gentlemen's club in the city centre where Cha Cha worked as a dancer; or more to the point a lap dancer.

Cha Cha was sweet and very unlike any of the other girls he had taken as fares from The Glass House. In his own words 'she was posh totty!' Hard to age because of the hair and makeup; Mark thought her to be about 22, she was in her last year at University so couldn't have been much younger. Privately educated and hailing from somewhere down south; she talked like she was part of the Royal Family. Not at all what you would expect to be gyrating their body for money in a lap dancing club.

But Mark liked her and over the months they built up a bit of a friendship. Like Jason Lee; Cha Cha knew all about Anna and the baby. Mark in return knew very little about Cha Cha apart from that she wanted to eventually be a teacher and she was living away from home. The Glass House was to help fund her independently through University; she didn't want any help from her parents; but Mark never asked why.

Cha Cha was struggling though; the dancing and the assignments were weighing heavy on her. Totally out of character; Mark suggested a little upper one night on the journey home; just one to keep her awake long enough to finish her assignment and meet her deadline.

Handing it over he stressed he had no idea what it was; all her knew that it would help keep her awake. They were called 'Fool's Gold!' The warnings should have been in the name; but Cha Cha took it off him gratefully and handed over her money.

Mark felt like a shit. He liked Cha Cha. But business was business and he pushed the £10 note she handed over into his jacket pocket along with the rest of the night's takings.

Cha Cha had hit her deadline. And then she hit her purse for more.

That was the beginning of Cha Cha's demise. Mark could understand why she was doing it. But the more she bought the more hours she had to work at The Glass House; Cha Cha had literally stepped on to the hamster wheel Mark had got himself off by dealing the drugs.

It was a dog-eat-dog life.

In no time she was handing over all of the money she had earned at The Glass House the minute she stepped out of the building and into his taxi. Mark hated it. He hated handing over the 'Fool's Gold' and he hated giving her a lift home. But what else could he do?? If it wasn't him then it would be another supplier and they would charge her more and give her God knows what?

It went on for so long. Cha Cha was skin and bone. She was a shadow of the young dancer who had first hopped into his taxi. It was his doing!

And yet still he not only supplied Cha Cha, but so many others. But there was only Cha Cha who haunted him. The rest were faceless.

And during all the madness of the taxi and shenanigans there was India.

Every day she amazed him. He was the proudest dad in the world and somehow having India justified why he was living in all the madness. India and Anna.

They would be needing to move out of the little one bedroomed flat in the city centre soon. It was getting too small and it would be nice to get somewhere with a garden for the toddling India.

If he kept the business going for another 6 months he would manage a move and still have a little bit left for emergencies. He could keep the taxi up and get rid of the side hustle. But it wouldn't be easy; both businesses ran through the same mobile number. But still!

Then bang. It was over!

Mark had just dropped off a punter and was pulling out of a side street when someone crashed in to him. He woke up days and days later in hospital; he had taken a nasty bump on the head and the police had taken possession of his drugs. The punter hadn't been a punter that he had just dropped off; he was one of Jason Lee's men who had been in the taxi to replenish Mark's stock.

At his hospital bedside, Mark had been arrested.

Anna was mortified. She'd had no idea. Her emotions ran from angry to remorseful within one sentence. It was her doing; she had pushed him into it all. She hadn't though; he was a grown man with responsibilities and had realistically taken the easy route.

His mobile telephone which would without doubt lead to a custodial sentence had never been found. The drugs were the only thing that was found in the taxi.

The mystery of the missing mobile phone made his already hurting headache more. The thought of going to prison made his already hurting head spin. But all he could do was wait and see what the police did next and hope that he would be released to go home.

Anna enlightened him about the missing phone; it had been in his jacket pocket and Anna had seen it and kept it out of the way. With the hospital happy that there would be no lasting damage beyond the headaches; Mark was free to go home into Anna's care.

The police came and took a statement. No he had no idea where the drugs came from. No he had no idea who the fare had been before the crash. And no he had no idea where his mobile phone was.

Mark was still under arrest and the police said that

they would be back.

The headaches grew worse.

Anna gave Mark his mobile phone; It was dead. He did wonder about Cha Cha; what would have happened to her? He threw the mobile in the bin and the headaches got worse.

Mark took to his bed; he had little patience with himself never mind anyone else.

The police returned. All charges were dropped. They had no evidence to prove that he had drugs with the intent to supply. It was over!

The relief to both Mark and Anna was tangible.

Anna had stood by Mark when she really didn't need to. She should have run for the hills with India; it was no secret that Mark had been arrested for supplying drugs; everyone knew. But Anna had stayed by his side and how he loved her for it.

Mark actually loved Anna.

Mark would not be going back to be a taxi driver; the police would have their beady eyes on him, but he needed to do something. They had the insurance money from the taxi write off and they had a little savings but the rent on the flat was mammoth.

There was nothing else for it but for them to move out of the city centre into a bigger cheaper property.

And just as they began their search an unexpected windfall fell in their laps. A package was hand delivered to Mark. Inside was £10,000. Mark knew instinctively that it was from Jason Lee. There was no note. But Mark knew. It was a thank you for keeping quiet.

It was dirty money; but it was the new beginning Mark, Anna and India needed and they were not going to look a gift horse in the mouth.

It was a no brainer. They found a house about 10 miles outside of Newcastle; Mark bought himself a van; booked himself on to a refresher course to be an electrician and that was it. They had their new beginning.

There had been only one thing Mark had wanted to do before he got the hell out of dodge. He went to The Glass House.

Mrs Glass had not been very forthcoming when she first spoke to her. But she must have seen the genuine concern for Cha Cha because she warmed to him and was soon telling him a brief outline of Cha Cha and her morphing into Lindsey.

Mark was barely listening. All he knew was that Cha Cha had not died. He left with a spring in his step. They had both survived the madness.

They had both been given a second chance and for Mark he never looked back.

Theo was born within a year of moving into their new home. A daughter and now a son.

His electrical business was doing ok; working for himself was as scary as it had been on the taxi; but they cut their cloth accordingly.

Jason Lee's money was in the bank for an

emergency; but if they did dip into they put it back. It really was for a rainy day but just having it there took the pressure off them.

Anna passed her exams and became a personal trainer; this time she worked for herself and booked in sessions around the children and Mark.

They could not have been happier.

Even when the pandemic came and they couldn't work; they saw it as an 'at home' holiday and made the most of being together. They may be made too much of the time; by the time they went into the winter lockdown and Mark was back out working; Anna was pregnant again.

Another boy; this one Sonny because he had been conceived in the sunniest days in the bleakest of times during the pandemic.

And that is basically Mark Dickens. Father of three. Partner of Anna. Electrician running his own business. Mark Dickens living the peaceful life he always wanted when he realised he was never going to be the next Alan Shearer.

And then there was that parents evening. India's teacher; Miss Kinghorn.

Miss Kinghorn who India talked about all the time. Miss Kinghorn this and Miss Kinghorn that! India was in awe of her. ' We hard work with her but lots of fun things too!' India would say.

Mark had seen Miss Kinghorn when he had been on

the school run; but not long after going into Miss Kinghorn's class; India decided that she didn't want her mam or dad picking her up from school. So Mark or Anna would pick Sonny up from nursery; Theo up from the infants and then wait patiently in the car for India to make her own way out of school. Miss Independent!!

The parents evening was the first time that Mark and Anna would speak to the illustrious Miss Kinghorn.

Mark didn't particularly like parent's evening; he hated his kids being weighed and measured. But Anna had insisted and took his seat by her side in front of Miss Kinghorn.

Anna introduced them as India Dickens parents.

Miss Kinghorn spoke and Mark nearly fainted. That voice.

He knew that all the colour had drained from him face; Anna must have realised something was up to because she did all of the talking while Mark sat and gawped at Miss Kinghorn.

Mark would have known the voice anywhere. The face not so much. But as he stared; Miss Kinghorn caught his eye and he knew instantly that she knew he knew.

Cha Cha!!

He could not believe it. The fresh faced; pretty young teacher that his daughter talked about; well more than talked about; adored was Cha Cha.

Appointment over; he literally had no idea what Miss Kinghorn had said about India.

Anna on the other hand wanted to know what was going on the minute they were out of the building.

After Mark had been arrested for drug dealing there had been no more secrets between him and Anna. He had told her all about how it began; the punters; the dealings and of course Cha Cha.

It had been Anna's suggestion that he went back to The Glass House. She said he needed to have some sort of closure or at least peace of mind before they left the city. It had been the right thing to do. Anna knew beyond friendship there had been nothing going on. Mark Dickens may have been a drug dealer but he was not a cheat. Miss Kinghorn being Cha Cha was unbelievable.

Anna insisted that they stay and talk to Miss Kinghorn. If Mark had recognised her then surely she would have known who he was too. 'And what if she takes against India?' Mark agreed. He had to face up to her.

So, they waited and waited and eventually she came out of the building.

If Mark thought that there was going to be some sort of confrontation, he could not have been more wrong. It was much more Friends Reunited!!!

It was hard for Anna to work out who had apologised the most!

By the time they parted company for their own cars; it was done. They agreed that there would be no hard feelings. What had happened had ended up being the making of them both. Mark couldn't believe that she had married the Manager of The Glass House; that Mrs Glass was at her house now looking after her little boy!

If there had ever been a slight shadow on Mark Dickens life; Cha Cha had been it. Seeing her as Miss Kinghorn; her achievements despite everything she had gone through made him feel a little bit like when India walked for the first time; or Theo said Daddy or he found Sonny's first tooth. A proud father! Cha Cha had done good.

The shadow had gone. Miss Kinghorn would likely be in their lives for some time yet to come; there were still the boys to go through the primary school and for Mark that was somewhat of a comfort.

£10 note HE75 229564 had not directly affected Mark Dickens life. It was just one of the many notes that went through his hands and through the electric gates of the Lodge.

A shady deal in a dodgy time when life was mad and cash was king!

'Rock Bottom Became a Solid Foundation on Which I Rebuilt my Life.'

J K Rowling

12

The Best That Money Can Buy!

Jason Lee had been Mark Dickens Grand Master. He had been the person that suggested to Mark that he could help him bolster his taxi driving income. Jason Lee had been the man that had showed Mark the ropes, supplied him with merchandise and in return Mark had paid him handsomely. And that is how £10 note HE75 229564 came to be in Jason Lee's possession.

Not that Jason Lee would have noticed the £10 note even if it had been gold plated. It was just one of many.

But as many people as he had working for him; there wasn't a man that he knew as well as Mark Dickens.

When Jason Lee had lost his driving licence for having one drink too many one night; Mark had taken on the role as his regular taxi driver. It wasn't a long journey home from Jason's city centre club to his home on the outskirts of town; but over the months; Jason and Mark developed a friendship. When he had seen the young taxi driver struggling to make money; Jason had suggested doing a bit work for him. It resulted in a very lucrative bit of business for both of them.

But then there had been the crash which resulted in

Mark Dickens being hospitalised and arrested simultaneously and that had been the end of the partnership. But Mark Dickens had kept stum even when faced with jail time, Jason was impressed; many would have buckled under the pressure. When there was no decent amount of proof that Mark was dealing had been found; the charges had been dropped and Jason Lee made sure that whatever Mark Dickens did next; he had the means to do it.

Jason Lee admired and rewarded loyalty.

But for some time after Mark's accident; Jason missed the friendship, even thought about looking for him; they may have had shady dealings going on; but they still managed to put the worlds to right in the 15-minute journey they made across town.

If the truth be told Jason Lee didn't have a lot of friends. He had acquaintances; people he had known through business for years. People who he didn't mind going for a meal with; a round of golf or even with their partners to some function or another. But they weren't really friends. Jason Lee wouldn't trust any of them.

Friends he'd had from his youth had fallen along the wayside as he began to climb the ladder; they either wanted something for him or they resented his success. Jason Lee could never understand why they would resent him; if it had been any of his school friends he would have been over the moon for them. Or would he?? Jason had worked hard for his success; driven and focused he hadn't really taken much notice of what went on around him. Would he have been different if he'd had a regular job; if he'd been the one working 40 hours a week for a pittance and one of his good mates had taken flight. It had been a dilemma he had never needed to face.

Nowadays he couldn't even imagine inviting any of his old school friends to his house; not like he had when they had been kids. His house had always been an open door; after all they had nothing worth stealing. So, there had always been a steady stream of kids that didn't live there calling in for him or one of his brothers or sisters.

If his dad wasn't there that was. Billy Lee the old bastard; that beat his wife and kids and took any money they had for themselves. The old bastard had lived to be 95! How had that happened when his wife had died so young. But then Billy Lee had been the giver of punishment and not the taker. Jason hadn't seen his dad for a very long time; even when the family had told him he had gone into residential accommodation Jason hadn't gone; he hadn't given his dad a penny towards his care. But Jason would have given his mam the world; if she had been around long enough to know that Jason could afford to give her it.

What would his mam had made of the Lodge. Jason Lee knew fine well what his mam would say 'Our Jason; what do you need a house that big for, nowhere near the shops even. You're just showing off!' and she would have been right.

The Lodge was a status of how far he had come. Not that the house had been his idea; when he acquired the land he had been just going to sell it on; but his second wife Amanda had cajoled him into showing it to her and any thought that he had of making a quick few quid selling it were out the window.

Because what Amanda wanted Amanda got.

He had heard the whispers; Amanda being a gold digger and only after his money. It may have been true; in the beginning anyway. Like himself, Amanda had come from nothing. But she had proved over and over again that she was no dumb blonde. First she had helped him revamp the city centre club into somewhere that everyone wanted to be seen. And then she took on the Lodge.

Spade by spade and brick by brick; with the help of the builders, she had made the bit of waste land into a palace. The house; the gardens; all Amanda's foresight. And she had been savvy with the costs too. It was unbelievable howe much profit was tied up in the gated perimeter of his home.

But Jason Lee had always hated the Lodge.

Not the house itself; that was stunning. It was just the house. It gave him the willies and the shivers and every other thing that made you feel uncomfortable. It was like the house had eyes! For a man the size of a house himself; it made him feel pathetic. Everyone else loved it, none more so than Amanda; it was her pride and joy.

With the arrival of their daughter; January and his granddaughter Maddie; the house seemed to be happier. For Jason, the walls weren't so oppressing and the sound of the girls was the only thing that seemed to make his spine tingle; but that was with excitement and not fear. Those two little girls were his life.

Jason had missed out on so much when his first daughter had been born. He was so busy building his empire that he had little time for little Olivia; her care was left to Paula, his long suffering first wife. When the girls had been born only a couple of days apart; he vowed that this time he would get it right.

He was king of his empire. The legal and the illegal one. Jason Lee had everything he could possibly want bar one thing. Peace of mind.

In Jason Lee's mind it was a younger man's game. Not that it would be easy untangling himself from it all; but for January and Maddie he would do it. He didn't want to miss a minute of them if he could have helped it.

In his office at the Lodge, he had made himself an exit route.

Assets he could sell, including the city centre club, the Lodge and the luxury apartment that he had bought years ago. But there were lots of other smaller properties that he could off load.

They had a place in Marbella. If need be they could go live there for a while. Amanda loved it there and didn't mind taking the girls over there on her own for a week or two.

But Jason hadn't spoken to Amanda about selling the Lodge; there just had never been the right time.

In theory they could all live a comfortable life;

Amanda, Livvy and the girls way beyond when he had shuffled off the earth.

He was in a precarious position though. The merchandise he sold for one would set off alarm bells ringing if anything changed. It would all have to be managed meticulously; it was such a lucrative and dangerous business that it would all need to be handled with kids gloves; especially if he was going to hand the reins over to his right hand man. In Jason's head it made sense; Tom Holmes had been a loyal employee and confident.

It had all been food for thought.

It would be a conversation to be had with Amanda, the legal bits anyway. He knew she wasn't green and that he had his hands in lots of pies; he just didn't want her to think badly of him. Drug dealer wasn't a badge he liked to wear. Drug dealers did bad things and he had been no different.

But he was different. His heart wasn't in it anymore and if his heart wasn't in it then he would take his eye off the ball and before he would know it he would be in Durham serving a very long sentence.

Amanda and the girls didn't deserve that. He had almost lost Amanda once due to his deceit; he wouldn't be risking it again.

That was something else that gave him the willies; he didn't like to think about it. Overnight his vivacious wife turned into a shadow of herself. She totally shut down; wouldn't talk to him, wouldn't touch him. He had no idea what was going on and he was scared.

Amanda was the woman of his dreams. He had fought so hard to win her over. He had left his wife and his daughter to be with her and when she had eventually agreed to marry him he was the happiest man on earth. To him, Amanda was a goddess and even if people thought that his young new wife was only with him for his money; then so be it. He was the one that she gave her beautiful body to time after time. She was the one that went on holidays with him. She was the one that he shared his life with. It was all just sour grapes!

But then she had done the whole change thing and he was beginning to get the feeling that she had somehow found out what he really did for a living.

To add salt to the wounds; Livvy his daughter became distant from him too.

Jason Lee had been beginning to think that Livvy was in love. She was so happy and so hyper. But then she too became distant from him. From the Lodge where she usually darted in and out of. Livvy had never been adverse of bring friends over and partying around the pool, Jason never worried about them getting up to no good; Amanda always had an eye on them.

So for a time he seemed to have lost Amanda and lost Livvy.

Jason was never sure if the thought of Amanda and Livvy finding out his business than the truth had been. At that point anyway.

They were pregnant. Both of them!

Jason Lee's world crumbled around his ears.

Livvy had been seeing the Lodge's gardener's son. But Drew Harrison had scarpered the minute he had found out about the baby. Jason had been furious and despite sending out a search party; there was no sign of the gardener's wayward son.

Livvy wouldn't hear of having an abortion. It was a fete au complete. Jason Lee was going to be a grandfather!

Worse still though was Amanda being pregnant. He truly did not know what to say to Amanda; he did not know how to make things better for her; for them!

She had said from day dot she didn't want kids. Her mam and dad had her when they were 16 years old; kids themselves. Then her brothers had arrived and it was kids bringing kids up; she just didn't want it. She had asked him if he would mind having a vasectomy; the pill didn't agree with her and the last implant she'd had made her gain weight.

Always wanting to make her happy he had agreed and went off to his private doctor where all the arrangements were made. But as big and as scary that Jason Lee was; he was terrified of needles; of operations and of doctors in general. So he had lied and said he'd done it and for years they hadn't got pregnant and that was just down to God and good Grace.

Now his lie had been revealed and that was why Amanda hated him.

Always a problem solver; Jason had no idea what to

do. All he could do was wait it out.

His life was purgatory. Livvy was so excited about her baby, she was under the illusion that her absent boyfriend would come back; but word was out that Jason Lee was looking for him; if the lad had any sense he wouldn't be coming knocking on Livvy's door anytime soon.

After what seemed like an eternity it was over. All thanks to two little photographs; one of his grandchild and the other of his child.

It was over.

Amanda was having the baby. The wall that had been surrounding her for all of those months came tumbling down and Amanda was back!

By the time January Lee was born quickly followed by Maddie Lee; all was well in the Lee household at the Lodge.

The thought of retiring was stronger than ever for Jason Lee though. With the arrival of the two little girls it became even more important for Jason to get out of the business; there were some nasty folk around him who may think a quick few quid could be made by kidnapping the children; it was a constant worry for Jason.

Maddie spent almost all of her time with Amanda; more so when Livvy went back to work and even more so when she picked up on her social life and the realisation that Drew Harrison would not be her knight in shining armour and come back and sweep her off her feet; she got herself a new boyfriend.

The day to day care of Maddie fell to her step grandma and himself.

January and Maddie were inseparable. They played together; slept next to each other and when they decided that they would go and dip their toe in the water and see how they would feel about spending more time at the villa in Marbella; Maddie went too.

All the while Jason worked on his exit route. Marbella really was starting to look like a feasible option. There would be a good English school for January when the time came; and Maddie too by the looks at it. They could live there quite comfortably. The villa was paid for and they would have enough money in the bank to give them a similar lifestyle as they had in Newcastle; with better weather and a healthier lifestyle.

Surprisingly Amanda thought it a good idea too. Motherhood seemed to have made her softer; she wanted the best lifestyle for the little girls and after the first holiday with the girls in Marbella; she would go backwards and forwards.

They had a Christmas at the villa. A big family one which included Livvy and her new boyfriend and Amanda's mam and dad; Claire and Mick. The latter lived in Jason Lee's apartment in the city centre; had done for a few years, rent free of course. If they were going to have to be turfed out of the apartment; then Jason would need them on side; he would see them all right, but wherever it was they ended up living it wouldn't be a patch on the top floor apartment they had that had views of the Tyne. It was going to have to be a big sweetener. As much as Amanda had complained about her upbringing; she adored her mam and dad; they were more like a big brother and sister than parents; so, it wouldn't do upsetting them and getting it in the ear off Amanda.

Christmas turned out to be much better than expected. For Jason Lee spending the majority of his time kicking back and relaxing, it felt good. He had left the majority of the responsibility of the businesses to Tom Holmes; it was like a test; see how he handled things on his own without constantly having to ring his boss. Jason's phone was quiet; either things at home had gone very wrong or Tom was coping.

When everyone returned home in the New Year; Amanda and the girls stayed behind. The villa needed a face lift and Amanda thought that winter would be the best time to do it and set about making the villa their home.

Then Covid-19 hit. Amanda; January and Maddie couldn't get home. There were no flights; no ferries; nothing.

Jason Lee tried everything to get his girls home but it was useless.

Lockdown arrived along with Livvy and Dean; her boyfriend. There was no way she was going to stay in her mam's little house when her dad had a swimming pool and a massive house. Jason was mortified and relieved at the same time. Staying at the Lodge on his own had filled him with dread; with the girls away the house had taken on its sinister ways again and Jason hated it.

Contact with Amanda was via Facetime and Zoom calls; but they were coping in Spain; the sun was shining and they were all spending their days out for walks and playing in the pool. Jason missed them all.

With no club to run; Jason's days were very different.

He wasn't worried about the club; the staff were to be furloughed and his accountant assured him that the Government funded money would be enough to sustain the business until it reopened.

The other business was his worry.

Demand went through the roof!

No one seemed to have anything else to do!

There was no end to it and the cash just kept on coming!

It was making Jason Lee nervous. Being at the Lodge he felt like a sitting target; the police; burglars. There was so many comings and goings. Usually supplies came in through the club and various small businesses around the city; but they were all closed and to re-open them without them being 'essential' businesses would be a red flag. So, everything was coming to the Lodge.

Livvy was oblivious to everything; she had been around her dad all her life and took no notice of anything he did. But the boyfriend was different. He saw the cars and vans come to the Lodge at all hours; knew that Jason would lock himself in his office for long period of time and that there was a safe in said office.

Jason had no choice but to tell Dean what it was all about; playing everything down as much as he could. Dean said he already knew what Livvy's dad did; he had worked in enough bars in the city centre to know the name.

Dean turned out to be an extra pair of hands; an extra set of ears and would keep an eye out whenever someone arrived at the bottom gate. Dean went onto the payroll and all of the time Livvy was oblivious.

The months ticked by.

Restrictions lifted a little; but not enough for Amanda and the girls to get home or Jason to get to them.

Business boomed and Jason Lee became more nervous.

He hoped that one day soon the supplies would run out; it beggared belief that supplies could get into the country when his wife, daughter and granddaughter couldn't. But the supplies just kept on coming and the sales went up and up and up. The safe was choker block with money; he couldn't even put it into the bank; the club was closed, there was no explanation as to where the money was coming from legally.

The exit route was becoming more and more tempting.

Property prices were through the roof; he could make a killing on all of them if he acted quickly.

He did and within days his portfolio was on the

market; including the city centre club. All he had to do was hang in a little longer. Pray that the police didn't come knocking or the tax man look too closely at what was selling and how he came by some of the smaller ones and then he would be on a plane; if there were any flying out and with his family in the Spanish sunshine.

If Amanda was shocked about what he had done; she didn't look it, in the fuzzy Zoom call anyway. There was nothing she could do to help; if the Lodge sold and she still wasn't back, then he would have to pack their things up and put them into storage.

The strange times suddenly became even stranger.

The offers came in thick and fast on the majority of the properties. Sold; sold; sold! The club had an offer made; which was surprising seeing as there was still no sign of when it would be able to reopen. The apartment sold; the sweetener was offered and taken; Amanda's mam and dad were now very affluent in their own right and never had to strike a bat to earn it. They even had the audacity to say they would book flights when they could and go out and join Amanda and the girls until they decided what they were going to do.

By the time Christmas came and they were in another Lockdown there was only the Lodge on the market. The asking price was eye watering so both Jason and the estate agents knew that it would take a little while longer.

After the previous Christmas it was a very quiet and sombre one. There was only Jason Livvy and Dean and the never ending cars and vans turning up at the Lodge.

They Zoom called Spain all of the time. The girls were so excited. If Livvy was peeved that Maddie seemed to be calling Amanda Mammy too she didn't show it. Like Jason hadn't seen his wife and daughter for almost a year; Livvy hadn't seen her daughter either!

An offer came on the Lodge in the New Year; full asking price. Jason was shocked; he thought that he would have had to drop at least a few thousand off. The prospective buyers hadn't even set foot in the place. Everything had been done using videos.

Amanda seemed a bit subdued when Jason rang to tell her the news. Jason put it down to the fact that the house she had built with her own fair hands was going. There was a completion date set for 3 months later; time for Amanda to maybe make it home one last time; help pack up the belongings and decide what was needed in Marbella and what could go into storage until they decided where they would be living.

She must have been quite upset about the whole situation as the phone calls and Zoom calls became more and more infrequent.

Jason was so embroiled in what was happening in Newcastle that he barely noticed. The prospective buyers on the city centre club upped their offer and Jason accepted it. That was the final piece of the jigsaw. Jason Lee's portfolio was now empty; the legal one anyway.

Now all there was to do was to speak to Tom Holmes about taking over the other side of the business and that would be all of the ties severed. Once the Lodge was completed it would be Viva Espana!

Tom Holmes had proved himself more that capable. He had all of his boss's hardness and business savvy with the edge of a much younger man. He had already made arrangements to move the supplies from the Lodge; with all the legal type people coming to survey the property and such like; they couldn't risk a van turning up. More often than not the driver didn't even speak good English and it resulted in a bit of a spectacle.

Livvy and Dean were still living at the Lodge. They didn't want to go to Marbella; Jason would find them somewhere to live. Dean had been working with Tom Holmes for quite some time and the two men made a formidable duo; Jason had the feeling that the shady business would continue to grow and thrive. Jason's only hope was that Dean didn't bring any trouble to Livvy's door; especially if little Maddie was living there too.

But there had been no noises off Livvy about going to collect Maddie or making a home for her when she did eventually get home. It seemed that Maddie calling Amanda Mammy was playing into Livvy's hands; Jason couldn't see Livvy being mammy to Maddie anytime soon. All her attention was on Dean and the life they shared and were going to share going forward.

Amanda couldn't make it home. Too many hoops to be jumped through with the girls. The tests they would need before they even set foot on a plane. Jason Lee thought it was more that she didn't want to come home to the Lodge; not when it was no longer going to be her home. He got that; it was her baby so to speak when she didn't have a baby of her own.

Jason enlisted her mam and dad to come and help pack up; Jason would have no idea what to do. Claire and Mick were about to leave the city centre apartment and were going to stay at the Lodge anyway; so it killed two birds so to speak.

All that remained was for the contracts to be exchanged; flights booked and they would be on their way to their new life.

Jason Lee was beginning to sleep soundly in his bed at night. The end was in sight.

The money stashed in the safe was slowly being loaded onto pre-paid cards that could be used in Spain; Jason was grateful that he had Livvy; Claire and Mick to help with them; for once Jason Lee wanted it to be done legitimately; he couldn't risk getting one of his associates doing the job for him. Nothing was being done that would muster up a red flag.

Jason Lee closed the Lodge gates behind him as he drove out of the long winding drive for the last time. All he had to do was drop the keys in with the solicitor and that was that. Hand on heart; Jason was not sad to see the back of the place and said it out loud to Livvy who thinking her dad may upset had said she would leave when he did.

'You never liked the place dad did you?' On the journey into the city centre Jason was telling her how the place gave him the willies; that he always felt he was being watched and had never rested easy. 'Mam said she wouldn't have lived there for all of the tea in China!' Livvy retorted. And then went on to tell her astonished dad about how the original Lodge; which had been part of a big estate had been burnt to the ground many years earlier. How the couple who lived there had been burnt alive!

Amanda had told her the story Livvy said. Years ago! It was a snippet of information that Amanda had failed to pass on to her husband. On retrospect it was probably the right thing to do; not tell him. The house would have been on the market years ago!

But it was all behind him now. He would be flying out of Newcastle Airport later that night. Claire and Mick; Amanda's mam and dad had already left on the morning flight. To be honest Jason had been pleased about that. He had been in Claire and Mick's company lots of times; the last time they were at the airport together they had got pissed and very loud. It had been a shock that they had even been allowed on the plane. They still hadn't grown up; probably never would. It was just their mentality.

And that should have been that. Jason Lee leaving his life in Newcastle behind him. Living in the Costa del Crime with all of the other hoodlums that decided they had sailed for too close to the wind and ducked out of the UK before anyone came to feel the necks of their collars.

£10 note HE75 229564 had very little effect on Jason Lee's life. Money came to him by the sack full.

By the time the plane had touched down in Malaga airport he felt like the weight of the world had been lifted off his shoulders.

Amanda had seemed distracted when he had spoken to her earlier in the day. Jason put it down to her very tipsy mam and dad arriving at the villa. But they had delivered the pre-paid debit cards with no drama; and they had gone out to celebrate the start of their holiday in town; Lord knows what state they would be in by the time Jason arrived.

Jason had refused the offer of Amanda picking him up from airport or sending a car for him; Jason was happy to jump in a taxi and travel like a tourist.

Travelling in the taxi made him think of Mark Dicken and the number of taxi rides they had taken together. He hoped Mark was happy. Mark and Anna and India. Jason congratulated himself for recalling all their names so quickly; he was getting on but his mind was still sharp.

It was late when he arrived at the Villa. Lights blazed out of every window.

It had been so long since he had seen Amanda, January and Maddie that his stomach did a little flip.

It had been so long since he had touched his wife. She was his Goddess. He hadn't even seen her yet and he had stirrings going on. Another little congratulatory note to himself; all his body parts seemed to be in working order.

Bursting through the door he expected to see an

expectant Amanda waiting for him. But the hallway was empty. As was the living room. The kitchen. The veranda. The patio. Thinking that maybe everyone would be upstairs he made his way up.

The villa looked very different to when he was there last. Everything had been given a lick of paint and looked new and fresh. There were some new paintings on the wall; all made by either his daughter or his granddaughter; they made the Villa feel like home. A nice touch by Amanda.

But the upper floor was empty too.

Where were they?

There didn't look like anyone had left in a hurry. One of the spare bedrooms had Claire and Mick's luggage in too, but there was no sign of them either.

Jason Lee made his way down to the kitchen. He took a bottle of white wine out of the fridge and poured himself a glass.

Sitting on the stool he called Amanda's mobile. Answer machine!!

Where were they??

Where was Amanda?? Where was January and Maddie?? Where were Claire and Mick for that matter??

Despite the heat of the night; Jason Lee shivered. There was something very wrong!!!

'Meet Me Where the Sky Touches the Sea!'
Jennifer Donnelly

13

Gold Digger

Amanda Lee was Jason Lee's so called trophy wife. The so called 'Gold Digger!'

And it was rightly so. Amanda had set her cap at Jason Lee. She had played a game of cat and mouse with the city centre club owner until all he could think of was Amanda. Before he had even laid a finger on Amanda; Jason Lee had left his long-suffering wife and child and set up home with the beautiful Amanda. For Jason Lee, Amanda was a Goddess.

He worshipped and adored her and bestowed everything he had on her. Car, clothes, jewellery, perfume, holidays and money; including £10 note HE75 229564.

As soon as he was able to he married Amanda and his life was complete.

Amanda Johns had been 19 years old when she decided that she was going to make Jason Lee her husband.

She knew all about him. He had quite the reputation in her home town. Notorious businessman and drug dealer. Jason thought she knew nothing of his shady dealings; but she knew much more that he had given her credit for. Including his reputation with young girls and women. They were easy come easy go to him. Amanda refused to be an also ran and from the onset she decided that the last thing she would do would be to jump into bed with him.

Before that happened he would need to be in love with her.

Amanda Johns was a wily one though. She knew what Jason wanted and needed and even after they married; she made herself indispensable to him. Not for the stuff she wasn't supposed to know about; but the club and other bits of business he had his fingers in. She gave Jason a new perspective on his business and in return he gave his wife the world.

Jason was over 25 years older than Amanda; he was actually older than her dad, but he was in shape and still a bit of a head turner. Amanda heard what people said; good time girl made good; gold digger; married her sugar daddy. It was true; but for whatever Jason gave to Amanda she returned two fold in different ways.

Amanda was an amazing stepmam to Jason's daughter from his marriage to Paula. At first it had been strained; Paula was stubborn about Livvy seeing her dad and his new bit squeeze as she called Amanda.

Amanda persevered though and soon Livvy was coming to stay weekends and then more and more in the holidays. Amanda fell in love with the little girl.

It was a priceless relationship for Jason; who thought he would lose his daughter when he married Amanda.

But Amanda had made it work; she had even talked Paula around into being a bit more hospitable. The new house had been Amanda's idea for Paula and Livvy to live in. It had a garden and was close to a good school for Livvy. No one suspected for a minute that Amanda would have suggested all of that because she had wanted to live in the 4 bed-roomed apartment in the city centre.

It always amazed Amanda how people only saw what they wanted to.

Jason only saw that Amanda fancied him. He never suspected that Amanda John had done her homework on him and knew exactly how to play him to get his attention.

Paula and Jason only saw that Amanda had found a home suitable for Livvy to live in which would have outside space for her to play in and a school within a stones throw away. They never suspected that Amanda had always had her eye on the apartment.

The Lodge had been Amanda's idea too. Jason had mysteriously come across a piece of land on the outskirts of town. Amanda knew the area well; she had often looked at houses in the estate agents windows and there was never any up for sale for anything less than a million. It was a perfect piece of land to build a house fit for the Lee family.

So she cajoled Jason to take her to see it and once she had she drew up sketches of what could be built there and the rest as they say is history.

It was a labour of love. Nothing got done without

her say so; every last detail was her decision; woe betide the builders if they decided to go off plan.

And how the builders hated her. She knew herself she was a first class bitch to them; in the beginning anyway. By the end they were all doffing their caps; her foresight had resulted in something magnificent.

Amanda and Jason moved in and Amanda's mam and dad moved into the apartment as caretakers.

Life couldn't get any better for Amanda. She had the home of her dreams; a man who adored her; a child to love who she ultimately only had to have fun with and had no responsibility for. And even though she knew that Jason didn't like living at the Lodge; she never took it upon herself to ask him; she didn't want him to say he wanted them to move.

Jason Lee would have died if he knew what had been on the land years before. But that was another snippet of information she would keep for herself.

They had a very good life together.

Until she met the gardener and Amanda's Lee's world turned on a sixpence.

Strictly speaking Drew Harrison wasn't her gardener; his dad was. But they had met and for the first time in Amanda Lee's life; she was in love.

It was unexpected; it was dangerous and it was all consuming.

Jason Lee would have killed them both if he had found out about them. But they were careful, they couldn't not be. To Amanda; Drew Harrison was the most beautiful human being that she had ever clapped eyes on. But it was an impossible situation.

Drew was young; a good many years younger than Amanda; unlike Amanda though; he had none of her savviness.

If Amanda had met Drew under any other circumstances, she would have called him a chancer; a player. He had little staying power for anything beyond Amanda. She wasn't green; he had history as young as he was; he couldn't be that good looking without having a string of women in his wake.

But Amanda and Drew were the real deal.

Just as well when she found out that she was pregnant to him. Well she had thought she was until Jason dropped the bombshell that he hadn't got the vasectomy he had booked in too many years earlier. It was a lie Amanda could not forgive him for; all the years when she thought that they were having safe sex he had been playing a game of chance with her.

The one thing that Amanda had said when they had eventually got together was that she did not want kids. Her mam and dad had been kids when they had her, quickly followed by her brothers; they had been a huge bunch of kids living together the best they could. It had been a hopeless situation and Amanda never wanted that for herself.

But he had lied to her. For years. Jason Lee shrunk in stature right in front of Amanda's eyes.

Jason's revelation did give her some breathing space though. She needed it because Drew Harrison had disappeared before she'd had chance to tell him she was pregnant. No it had not been Amanda Lee and her predicament he had run from.

No, it was Livvy Lee's predicament.

Somewhere, sometime; Livvy and Drew had met and had some type of relationship. All under Amanda's nose. She was so mad about it. Jason had asked her to find out what was going on with Livvy; she was avoiding her dad and hadn't been seen at the Lodge for weeks.

Amanda, traumatised by her own situation and at that point unaware that Jason had not gone for his operation was still working out how she was going to explain how she was pregnant when Jason was incapable. No one knew she was pregnant and the nausea that she felt every moment of the day and night was hidden away under a veil of her being depressed, agreed to go and see what was eating Livvy.

She hadn't been expecting baby news.

Livvy thought that Drew Harrison would be back. Amanda doubted it. Livvy Lee was Jason Lee's daughter; if he knew that Livvy was pregnant then he had run for the hills and wouldn't be back.

But Livvy had hope and Amanda couldn't agree or disagree with her. To all intents and purposes; Amanda barely knew Drew Harrison.

When Jason found out about Livvy he was furious. Not that she was pregnant so much; more that she had been left high and dry off some nobody. He would put word out about Drew Harrison. He would find him. Amanda knew he wouldn't. Drew Harrison had quite a big head start.

Amanda saw an opportunity with Livvy being in the house and dropped her bombshell too. This time the colour did drain out of Jason Lee's face.

There was nothing more to be said and for weeks Amanda pulled her make-believe veil of depression on and waited to see what happened next.

She walked the house like a ghost of herself; at least when Jason was around. When he wasn't she busied herself getting an exit plan ready. She opened herself a new bank account; in her name only and systematically sold as many of her belonging that she could without raising any suspicion. It was so easy and she managed to get herself quite a little fund in no time at all. But it wasn't enough to keep her in the lifestyle she had grown accustomed to; especially with a baby.

But it all kept her from walking the walls.

When Jason eventually told her he hadn't gone ahead with the operation she could have wept with joy. She had more time on her hands. She could make a proper plan. She could even stay put until after the baby was born.

It was bizarre. Jason could quite easily had been the father of the baby; she had been having sex with him too; there was no way she would risk him becoming suspicious that she her attention was elsewhere. But in her mind; the baby was Drew Harrisons; just like her step daughter's was.

January and Maddie Lee arrived two days apart.

Livvy had stayed at the Lodge with Amanda when they were nearing the end of their pregnancies. It made sense. Amanda even allowed Paula to come and stay; an extra pair of hands to come and fuss over the mini elephants.

It was living arrangement that stayed in place after the little girls were born.

They were like twins. Same hair colouring; same sort of size. It was only when you got to know them that you could see that they had slightly different face shapes. Jason was often confused between his daughter and his granddaughter.

When Livvy returned to work; Maddie stayed at the Lodge and Amanda became her main carer.

Again, it was a suggestion from Amanda. Go back to work Livvy; you need to get out with people your own age; Maddie is fine here. What Livvy didn't hear was that Maddie was Drew Harrison's daughter and she would be staying with her sister January. There was no doubt who January Lee's father was. Jason said both little girls were Lees' Amanda knew that both little girls were Harrisons.

And so, it began. Amanda became Maddie's mammy. As they got older and January started calling Amanda mammy; Maddie did too and Amanda didn't correct her.

They took January and Maddie to Marbella on holidays. Livvy never asked to come too. On the realisation that Drew Harrison was never coming back for them; she started dating again and met Dean who she seemed to get very fond of very quickly. She barely even rang to ask how her daughter were doing.

Jason started making noises about retiring. Maybe go and live in the Villa in Marbella! How did Amanda feel about that??

Amanda wasn't keen. But always happy to go out for a holiday; she agreed to go and spend some time at the villa and look at it as a potential permanent home.

It was a serendipity trip.

Amanda literally bumped into Drew Harrison when she had the girls out for their afternoon stroll. Shocked and stunned they agreed to meet up the following afternoon; and the afternoon after that and every afternoon until the holiday was over and the family returned to Newcastle.

By the time Amanda set foot down back in the UK; she knew that hers and the girls' future was with Drew Harrison. She just needs to work out how and when.

While she sorted out how she could get away with the girls she went back to the Villa many times. All on the pretence that she was getting a feel for living there. Sometimes she went on her own with the girls; sometimes she took her mam and dad and all of the time she saw Drew.

There was no repercussion about Livvy and Maddie. What could Amanda say; she had still been living her life with Jason Lee. Still went out with him; still holidayed with him. It was only natural that Drew would feel peeved. He just didn't realise for some time that the girl he got peeved with was Amanda's stepdaughter. It would be funny if it wasn't so tragic.

And it was obvious that Drew Harrison still loved Amanda Lee. He was totally in awe of her and even though they dared not get together alone; the electricity was shocking between them and they knew that if they timed everything just right; the rest of their lives together was theirs.

So, they bided their time.

Drew Harrison still had no money. He said he had a little bit of savings but his savings would be small change to Amanda and the money she was used to having. She need to box clever so when they did go; they had enough money to last them for a very long time. The chances of Drew becoming a Jason Lee was slim; even with Amanda's help.

They would wait and in the meantime she would fly backwards and forward all under the pretence of setting down some roots for the Lee family.

Amanda told Jason that they should spend Christmas in Marbella; a big family Christmas just like they would when they made the move. See how it felt; it was so important that January and Maddie had a traditional Christmas. Jason was up for it. But what Amanda had really meant was; I've not been to the Villa for a couple of months; I need to see Drew!

The family up sticks and all flew out to Marbella.

Amanda went all out; in her mind this would be the last Christmas they she and the girls would spend with Jason, Livvy and her mam and dad. She hoped against hope that by that time the following year they she would be in America with Drew and the girls. Because Amanda had decided that even though Maddie Lee wasn't her daughter; there was no way she would leave her behind. Maddie barely knew her mammy; Amanda was the one that cared for her. And January and Maddie were like peas in a pod; inseparable and capable of scrapping like a couple of street urchins.

The ace that Amanda had up her sleeve was that Drew Harrison was named as the father on Maddie Lee's birth certificate.

With so many others staying at the Villa it was almost impossible to see Drew. After two failed attempts where either her mam or Livvy came out for the afternoon stroll; Amanda decided that she would stay on in Spain when the rest returned to Newcastle.

Citing maybe getting the decorators in whilst the resort was quieter; Amanda, January and Maddie stayed on when the rest of the family flew back.

Now she could see Drew; at her leisure.

Then just like the rest of the world; Covid 19 came and Amanda, January and Maddie were trapped in Marbella.

No flights in and no flights out for the foreseeable future. The world was in limbo.

All the restaurants; cafes; shops and pubs closed.

Only supermarkets remained opened.

The villas around theirs remained empty; no holidaymakers came; there were only the ex-pats still in the area. At first the quietness made Amanda nervous. The Villa was some size and the tiled floors and walls made everything echo. She thought of Jason while she lay in the bed with her ears strained to hear if there was something in the Villa. The Lodge had always spooked him. But it would be nothing and very soon she got used to the silence outside; she couldn't grumble really, the amount of times she had complained because one of the neighbours was having a party and the music and car doors went on for most of the night.

Then there was Drew.

The casino where he worked closed down and he had a lot more time on his hands.

Feeling braver and with no cafes to sit in; they would walk the sea front pushing the double buggy. The chances of them bumping into someone who knew them was still there; but with everything else that was going on it didn't faze them as much.

If word got back to Jason Lee in Newcastle then it was one of those happy coincidences.

When the UK went into a full lockdown Amanda knew that there was no chance of Jason or any other family member just turning up; she took Drew back to the Villa and into her bed.

January and Maddie were used to seeing him. Amanda made sure that she always called him Andy when they were about and soon they were calling him Andy too.

It was daft Drew staying in his flat. She had a huge place and it looked like it was going to be a long time before they opened up the borders. It made sense him moving in with Amanda and the girls. The only thing they had to be careful of was the Zoom calls that Jason and Amanda had; sometimes Livvy and seldomly her mam and dad. But they got smart and Drew would make himself scarce along with any of his belongings that may give his presence away.

It was like an extended holiday.

They played in the pool; they went for long walks; they shopped at the local supermarket and ate on the patio.

Drew would help bath the girls and then tuck them up in bed and when they were settled Amanda and Drew would sit on the veranda, drink wine or beer or vodka and they would make their plans for the future.

At the end of the night they would stumble into bed and get to know each other's bodies all over again.

Amanda Lee had never been happier.

Drew Harrison had never been happier.

With Jason Lee safely back in Newcastle Amanda and Drew got chance to get to know each other properly. There was no need to check over their shoulders for one of Jason's cronies to see them. There was never anyone there.

But they both knew that they were on borrowed time.

The pandemic wouldn't last forever.

At some point they would have to move on.

Every day they checked the Spanish news for updates on flights. There was never much to report.

They would watch the daily Downing Street briefing on Sky News every day. There was never much to report.

So, they carried on with their holiday. It was like a honeymoon for them. The more time they spent together the more sure they were about the future.

Drew was smarter than she had ever gave him credit for. Maybe they could start their own little business when they eventually put down roots; he certainly wasn't afraid of hard work. He looked after all the maintenance and gardens meticulously. Maybe that could be an option Amanda had thought to herself as she watched him trim the lawn in his shorts; his body lean and tanned. The older he got the better looking he got, in Amanda's eyes anyway.

And he was caring. Amanda knew how worried he was about his mam and dad. Covid 19 was running rife throughout the North East of England he hated the thought of anything happening to his mam and dad. He had sent word to them on a few occasions since he had moved into the Villa; but he wasn't even sure if the post was getting through.

Amanda thought about asking her mam to find out if they were ok. But her mam had loose lips and if she inadvertently said something to Jason about Amanda asking after their gardener and his wife he would wonder why the interest. She certainly didn't want any awkward questions.

Jason made sure that she always had plenty of money. She would withdraw it from the cash point and stash as much as she could away. Amanda had turned into quite a savvy shopper; she was now only spending a fraction of what she would have done if she had been there and Spain had been open.

Her savings continued to grow.

Jason called her to say that he was thinking of putting his property and business portfolio on the market. It was time he said. Amanda and the girls were his life; retirement in Spain seemed like a good idea.

Amanda was shocked. He had talked about doing it before but that's all it had ever been talk. Now he seemed serious. House prices were at a high and when he called back a few days later with the estate agents market value for the Lodge; it was eye watering.

Jason thought that Amanda was upset because the Lodge was going on the market. What Amanda was doing was thinking that the profit in the Lodge was her doing. If she hadn't built it and built it well for that matter; there would be no 6-digit profit to be made. That was her money. Or at least some of it was and she would figure out a way to make sure she got it.

And all the while Amanda, Drew, January and Maddie lived it up in the Villa. It was happy families.

Bit by bit Jason Lee's business empire was sold off. He would ring every few days with an update. He must have been so busy that he didn't notice that the regular daily phone call and Zooms were becoming more and more infrequent.

Amanda asked for money to decorate the Villa; she had managed to secure a decorator and a gardener. Jason sent her extra money. The gardens were already pristine and Amanda found some end of line paint in a local supermarket that Drew used to paint the Villa. The rest of the money went into the savings.

Slowly slowly she was collecting a stash.

Christmas was a bit weird. Not for the family in Marbella; it was the stilted Zoom call where at one point January shouted Andy and Amanda had to think fast on her feet and say it was a new teddy she had bought Jason Lee's daughter! The girls were getting just too good at talking!

The Lodge sold. For its asking price. Again Jason thought her upset. In truth Amanda didn't care. Jason thought she may be able to get home sometime in the next 3 months before completion date and help pack up. Amanda knew there was no way on earth she would be ever setting foot in the Lodge again. All Amanda could think of was how she was going to get her hands on the money.

When the city centre club sold, Amanda knew that their days at the Villa were numbered. The only thing left was the completion of the Lodge sale and then there would be no reason why Jason Lee couldn't come out to Spain and join his wife, daughter and granddaughter.

Amanda needed to up her game. Limited flights were beginning to resume; there would be no excuse for her to tell Jason not to come.

Any doubts she had about taking Maddie with her and Drew were put to bed when Jason said that he had bought Livvy and her boyfriend Dean a flat. There had been no mention of Livvy coming to Marbella to collect her daughter. All talk was of the new flat and Dean when she rang to ask how Maddie was doing.

And Amanda had no feelings about leaving Jason Lee.

They'd had some good years. She had been spoilt rotten off him; he had made a pig out of a sows ear. She didn't think he had ever cheated on her. On paper there was no reason for her to fall out of love with him and in love with someone else. But she had and Jason Lee wasn't a silly man; they had had it good but it couldn't have lasted forever. Jason was in his 60's and Amanda her 30's and no doubt if she hadn't met Drew Harrison then she may have carried on regardless. But she had and Jason Lee had told her the biggest lie when he said he'd had a vasectomy and hadn't. That was the ace up her sleeve. She just could never forgive him for that.

The God's of Fate had definitely sent her a gem with that one.

Nevertheless one thing Amanda did have a little bit of sympathy for Jason for was the arrival of her mam and dad to live at the Lodge when the apartment sold.

Even though it was only going to be for a short time and they were helping pack up, Amanda knew of old what a nightmare her mam and dad could be.

Any excuse to party and the Lodge always had plenty of alcohol to ensure that at the end of their days of packing; they would have partied around the pool. Jason would hate it!

The news that they were coming to have a holiday at the Villa while they decided what they were going to do with the money Jason had given them to get out of the apartment filled Amanda with dread.

The only silver lining was that they were going to be bringing some prepaid debit cards with them for safe keeping. Jason said it was cash from the club. Amanda knew different; each of the cards would have a tidy sum of money on them. It was playing into her hands.

Almost!

Her mam and dad had booked their flights; Amanda knew when they were coming. More surprising was that Jason had also booked his flight; the late flight the same day!

Amanda and Drew had their D Day!

It was time!

Arrangements were made.

There was a car at the Villa but it was Jason's car and it was registered in his name. Amanda and Drew went and bought a similar one; they registered it in Drew's name.

They packed up what they would need; stuff for the

girls; a suitcase each for Amanda and Drew. They were travelling light. On the day that her mam and dad were due to arrive; Drew left the Villa with the car. They would be leaving later in the day; the car was already packed and they were going to leave it in a car park not far away from the Villa; after all Amanda would be going to it on foot with the girls and their little toddling legs.

They had a key each and had agreed that once her mam and dad had arrived and everything was sorted she would give him a ring and they would meet at the car.

Drew had to go and collect some belongings from the casino. Amanda thought that he seemed relieved to be leaving the Villa with the imminent arrival of her parents.

By lunch time Claire and Mick Johns had arrived at the Villa.

They'd had a lovely flight; obviously taken advantage of every drinks round on the flight over and with a little bit encouragement from Amanda; happily, dumped their suitcases in one of the spare rooms and went off with their daughter in search of one of the only pubs that was open on the front.

Two hours later; Amanda left her mam and dad drinking shots and made her way back to the Villa to make herself a sharp exit.

It was almost tea time and Jason would be ringing. She needed him to ring; everything needed to be as normal as possible. Right on cue her mobile rang. No he didn't want picking up or a driver sorted; he would happily get a taxi and was so excited to see them all later.

Amanda did actually feel like a bit of a shit. Jason Lee had not seen his wife; daughter and granddaughter for over a year.

But the wheels were in motion and as the girls continued their afternoon nap in the buggy; Amanda ran upstairs and rifled through her mam and dad's suitcases.

Jason had told her that Claire and Mick were bringing the pre-paid debit cards with them. In his eyes they looked too sackless to be doing anything illegal; Amanda had to agree and it had worked. There were almost 200 cards stashed in their clothes.

Amanda left the suitcases as she had found them and took the cards; did a quick check of the house and pushing the buggy in front of her; made for the door.

Drew answered straight away.

It was time!

With the girls strapped into their car seats; she passed them snacks as she waited for Drew. The casino was on the other side of town and when Amanda had called him; she could hear voices; he had obviously still been there.

January wanted a wee. Maddie wanted one too. It was dark so she dangled each of the little girls outside the car until little rivers of wee squelched under Amanda's feet. No sign of Drew and it was getting late.

The girls started to winge. Amanda thought about starting the car and taking them for a little ride. But what if Drew came and the car was gone. So she passed them their dummies; something she had been weaning them off for months but still kept for emergencies.

Amanda sat in the car for 4 hours when her mobile bleeped. Drew!

Amanda I love you and my daughters with all of my heart. The past months have been the happiest of my life. But I cannot run away with you. Jason will never stop looking for us. He will kill me. He will probably kill you. We can't risk it. I know I am a coward. You are the best thing that has ever happened to me. Don't look for me because I won't be there. I am at the airport about to board a flight. I'm sorry about the money. Look after my girls and yourself. I luv u

Amanda read and re-read it. She called Drew's number but it was unobtainable. He had gone. Drew had run away again and left her January and Maddie. She had given Drew 5000 euros; big mistake.

The rage that she felt was unlike anything that she had ever felt before. The girls were crying in the back of the car but for Amanda there were no tears. Starting the car; Amanda headed out of Marbella and headed for the airport; with every kilometre she drove she could feel her heart begin to harden. The girls slept in the back of the car.

By the time she reached the airport she was calm.

She thought Drew smart but he wasn't. Sooner or later the cracks would have appeared. When they were in Newcastle and sneaking about it had been adrenalin fuelled fun. In Marbella it had been like serendipity Amanda and Drew meeting up again. The Villa had been like one great big holiday. None of them were real life situations.

Spinning the car around a roundabout at the airport; Amanda headed back for Marbella.

Amanda was always a logical thinker and by the time she pulled the car on to the Villa driveway she knew what she was going to say.

The girls were fractious, so she took them for a ride out in the car; she wanted to make sure that they were asleep before her mam and dad got back. 'You know how loud they get when they've had a drink!' The car: well the other one was making a peculiar noise and there was no garage open to look at it; it was easier to buy a different one ....' The suitcases and bags in car could be sneaked into the house....

Amanda Lee had an answer for everything. She had even gone and got the pre-paid debit cards out of her mam and dad's suitcases, just for safe keeping. There was no trace of Drew Harrison in the Villa. Amanda had made sure of that before she had left earlier that day.

The thousands of photographs on her phone could be downloaded into a file. As mad as she was; there was no way she could oblate Drew from her life. One day she would look at them.

If word got to Jason that there had been someone at the Villa; someone that Amanda blatantly walked around Marbella with; then she would face that when it happened; if it happened. Amanda and Drew had not been that interesting!! The girls would forget; especially with so many new faces at the Villa. It would pay Amanda to keep her mam and dad there as long as possible; her childish parents were always bundles of fun for January and Maddie.

Leaving the sleeping girls in the car; Amanda made for the front door. She could do this. This was the life she was born for. She had worked so hard for it and the trappings it gave her. Realistically it would never have worked with her and Drew. But opening the front door of the Villa her heart felt heavy and cold. She wouldn't be giving it away to anyone anytime soon and certainly not Drew Harrison if he ever had the audacity to come back!

She could have a good life with Jason Lee. They had so much money like £10 note HE75 229564 that they could live any type of life they wanted. It wasn't going to mend her broken heart but it would help.

'Jason Jason are you here … I'm home.'

'I am Called a Gold Digger All the Time. I Don't Care. There is Nothing You Can Do About What Other People Say!'

Anna Benson

14

Take the Money and Run

When Drew Harrison had received £10 note HE75 229564 it was part of a big deal for him. He had to make a sharp exit and hapless Amanda Lee had handed him the note along with a few others. It was small change for her; but it made a difference for Drew; it allowed him freedom.

Hapless wasn't a word he would ever use to describe Amanda Lee. She was smart and savvy and oh so very sexy. Drew had never met anyone like her. The look of her; the smell of her; the taste of her. As enthralled as Amanda Lee was with Drew; he was double enthralled back. But in that moment; the moment that he 'borrowed' £50 off Amanda that would enable him to buy a train ticket to somewhere that wasn't Newcastle she was hapless to him.

He had screwed up big time.

Amanda: wife of one of the biggest Mr Big's in Newcastle was his lover. The heady mix of sneaky sex sessions with the trophy wife of Jason Lee had been intoxicating. The danger of being caught. The smugness of getting away with it kept Drew on his toes. And kept Drew interested.

Drew whose boredom threshold was so small that usually by the time he was climbing out of his latest conquest's bed; he had already lost interest.

Amanda Lee had been different. Drew left her bed already thinking when would be the next time he could see her. He couldn't get enough of her. But it was a dangerous game.

But it obviously wasn't dangerous enough for Drew and he had to add even more drama in to his life. Livvy Lee. Livvy Lee; Jason Lee's daughter from his first marriage. Amanda Lee's stepdaughter.

It hadn't been something he had planned. It had been a knee jerk reaction when Amanda had gone on holiday with Jason and left Drew high and dry.

Huffing massively that she had gone and not kept in touch like she said she would; Drew had taken himself out for a night out with his mates and slept with a girl. That girl turned up weeks later at the Lodge; the place where Drew worked with his dad on the gardens. Panicked when Livvy recognised him; he had asked her out.

It had started out as prevention control. There was no way he wanted Amanda to know that he had slept with someone when she was away; she had rang and she had text and as soon as she landed home; everything went back to normal; or as normal as their normal was. Drew wouldn't risk her stepdaughter opening her mouth and revealing his indiscretion. Then there had been her dad. Jason Lee surely wouldn't be happy with her having anything to do with the gardener.

Livvy Lee had agreed that it would be better to keep things to themselves. Happy that their secret was safe; Drew saw more and more of Livvy. She was sweet and funny and whereas Amanda was snatched moments; Livvy and Drew had a bit more freedom and spent days and nights together.

It was a very dangerous game Drew Harrison was playing. Something had to give!

That happened when Livvy announced she was pregnant.

If it had been Amanda that was pregnant he knew that the result would be no baby. Being a mother just wasn't on her radar. Livvy was different. Drew knew without a shadow of a doubt that Livvy would keep the baby.

There would be questions. 'Who's the daddy??' Livvy would expect Drew to stand up and stand beside her.

That could never happen. Amanda would burn him alive.

Amanda might have been smart and sexy and savvy; but at the end of the day she was a woman and no woman liked to have the man they loved infidelity thrown in their face. Added to that there was Jason Lee!!

Repercussions from Amanda were bad enough; Jason Lee's wrath was something Drew couldn't even think about. He would end up at the bottom of the Tyne wearing concrete boots.

The only thing Drew could do was the bastards trick and run.

He had run fast and he had run far.

First London and then he dotted about Spain; all with an eye on the door in case someone was looking for him. Drew was in no doubt that word would be out. Jason Lee would have contacts everywhere.

Drew Harrison became knowns as Andy Harris; gave himself a bit of a back story and got on with his nomadic life as well as he could.

Every now and again he would get word to his mam and dad. Never giving them a clue where he was; he just liked to give them peace of mind that he was alive. No doubt they would know all about Livvy Lee and the mess he had left behind. He prayed that he hadn't left them in a ton of trouble.

Andy Harris was very like Drew Harrison. He quickly reverted to how he was before Amanda and Livvy. It was all girls girls girls. They were a distraction, because if the truth be known; Drew was lonely. He missed his life in Newcastle. His mam and dad; his friends; he even missed the weather.

So he consoled himself in the arms of whatever female took his fancy, which was most females. In the sunshine of Spain there was always a steady supply. It was a quick fix; a high! But after every high there was a low. The lows lasted much longer than the highs did. It was a rollercoaster that Drew couldn't get off.

If he had been at home he might have sought out a doctor; but in Spain; living under a false name it wasn't an option.

The only thing he could do was work hard; try to wear himself out so that at the end of the night he was dog tired and not sought out the arms of some woman. But he worked in a bar and there was always someone. His workmates thought he was living the dream; for Drew it was more of a nightmare.

When a job opportunity came up in a casino Drew jumped at the chance. A new resort; a new type of job. A change was what he needed.

So he packed up his meagre belongings and headed for Marbella.

At first he was a bit nervous; Marbella was the place that Jason Lee played; he had a villa there. An eye on the door was even more important than ever.

But a year into the job there had been no sign of Jason Lee. Andy Harris remained a person of no interest to anyone in Marbella. Drew started to relax. The women were still there; it wasn't so much the quick fix anymore; he just liked women. Any type. But nowadays he did it more for pleasure and less for escapism.

He had a bit of a social life with people he worked with; had a decent little flat to live in and he actually loved his job. Every day was different and the nature of the job kept him on his toes; he was good at it and slowly began to climb the croupier ladder.

For once Drew thought that maybe he could lay down his roots in firmer foundations.

And then the earthquake came!

Amanda Lee. He saw her before she saw him. Caught off guard; he let the moment pass. He was far too shocked to be able to face her. Shocked to see her; shocked to see she was as beautiful as ever. Shocked about the feelings that she stirred up in him. But the biggest shock was that she was pushing a buggy with two little girls in.

The following day he went back and sat in the same café as the previous day and waited. Sure enough Amanda walked past again. By the third day he had orchestrated a 'happy accident' so it looked like it was a chance meeting!

It was all that was needed and Amanda Lee was back in his life again.

For the following weeks they met up every afternoon in some café or other. He had thought that she wouldn't have given Drew the lickings of a dog about the whole Livvy thing; but she hadn't; leaving Livvy pregnant had been a bit of a blessing in disguise for Amanda Lee.

To find out she had been pregnant too was a shock. More a shock that the two little girls in the buggy; the two very beautiful little girls with strawberry blonde hair were his daughters. Not twins but sisters. One by each of the Lee girls. It was a total head fuck.

Seeing Amanda Lee was like going home.

By the time she left for Newcastle they knew that they wanted to spend the rest of their lives together.

Drew was in no position to facilitate it; it was all going to be down to Amanda; she had the means at her finger tips; they couldn't live on fresh air. Moreover they would need to be careful; Jason Lee would be hunting them down; they needed to move fast and they needed to move far away. Amanda said she knew what she needed to do; he had to trust her.

What choice did he have? His feelings for Amanda were the real deal. Overnight the other women stopped. He had little interest in them. He hadn't even had opportunity to kiss Amanda never mind sleeping with her; but just being around her and having her back in his life was enough.

Drew would wait patiently.

Amanda was as good as her word. She kept returning to the Villa and to their furtive meetings. He was disappointed that even when she didn't have Jason Lee with her; Amanda still didn't invite him to the Villa. It was always an afternoon meeting; with the girls in their buggy in the shade and Amanda and Drew sipping on dubious coffee in cafes.

But the plans were coming along swimmingly. Amanda knew what to do; how to do it. It was just a matter of when and that was dependent on how much money Amanda could squirrel away. Time, they had! Drew could wait.

And then time was all they did have. Any thoughts of getting out of Spain were scuppered. The Covid 19 pandemic put paid to that. Overnight the borders closed; flights stopped and for once the God's were on their side. Amanda, January and Maddie were all trapped in Spain.

Jason Lee tried everything to get his girls home. It was useless. Jason Lee's misfortune turned out to be Drew Harrison's fortune. Within a couple of weeks Amanda had asked him to go and stay with her and the girls at the Villa.

Drew Harrison had the best year of his life.

The Villa; Amanda; January and Maddie!

It was the first time Amanda and Drew got chance to be themselves. There was no need to keep checking over their shoulders; Marbella was virtually deserted.

Jason Lee was stuck in Newcastle and there was no way he could pay them a surprise visit. Contact was all telephone calls; Facetime and Zoom. Drew would always make himself scarce.

If life was going to be like that with Amanda; one long joy ride, then he was all in.

With no work, their days were spent around the pool; or under the veranda in the shade. Every minute that passed Drew fell more and more in love with not just Amanda but with January and Maddie.

Drew could not comprehend how he had made such beautiful girls; to him they were perfect; and so alike. It had even taken Drew some time to work out which one was which; but once he had seen the difference he couldn't unsee it.

Personality wise January was the boss. She was the more confident, the dare devil. Maddie was more timid;

but what she lacked in confidence she made up for in cuddles. Maddie was definitely the care giver. Drew loved them so much.

And all the while Amanda continued to stash the cash.

Drew did jobs around the Villa; Amanda would tell Jason she had brought a bloke in to do it. Jason would diligently send the money; Drew would do the job and Amanda would put the cash with her growing stash.

When Jason rang and said he was going to sell his portfolio of property and business Amanda had been furious. The Lodge had been her baby; her home. But then she thought about it and realised that the profit from the Lodge was rightly hers and deviated ways to which she could get her hands on it. If Amanda could manage to get that; then the little family would be set for life.

Everything was coming together nicely.

Restrictions were beginning to lift and it was only a matter of time before Amanda was summoned home or Jason put in an appearance at the Villa. By all accounts Jason Lee was very much looking forward to his new life in Spain; Drew felt sick at the thought of Jason Lee's new life in Spain and the absence of his family!!

The Lodge sold. They had three months and counting. Jason had wanted Amanda to go home and pack up. She feigned that it was too difficult still. Jason Lee made no noises about coming out to Spain earlier. But still.

The escape plan was in place. They had even bought

a car; Drew had never had a car before. He had never been in a position to buy one; even on finance. He had never been good with money and had a credit report that proved it. God knows what shape it was in; he had not just walked away from Newcastle and his credit cards. Any car he had driven had been his mams or his dads. With the car in his name; he had valeted to within an inch of its life.

They packed up the Villa.

By the time the day came that they were leaving; they had everything they needed packed in the car and there was no trace of Drew Harrison ever spending a night at the Villa; in actual fact he had been there well over a year.

Amanda's mam and dad would be arriving early. They were bringing some pre-paid card things that Jason Lee had put some of his cash on. Amanda was going to take them and that would add to the pot they already had. Drew had no idea how much money would be on the cards; Amanda just said a lot. They were untraceable; that was the reason Jason had done it that way; but if they were untraceable for Jason Lee they would be untraceable for Amanda Lee too.

Jason Lee would be arriving in Malaga later that night.

Amanda told Drew not to worry; she had it sorted. She could distract her mam and dad; just the mention of a pub would be enough and she would have them out of the Villa. Amanda would take the cards they had brought with them and as soon as she heard from Jason when he got to Newcastle airport; they would go.

They parked the car in a car park not too far from the Villa.

Drew was disappearing for the day. Amanda would ring him when it was time; they both had car keys. He would just have to make his way back to the car.

Amanda had given him some cash to carry; she didn't want to be walking the streets of Marbella with bundles of it. The majority had been deposited into her bank account, the account she had set up years earlier when she found out she was pregnant and thought she was going to have to make a sharp exit. An account Jason Lee knew nothing about. With the prepaid cards; they had a tidy sum.

Drew was going to the casino. It was due to re-open the following week and he took the opportunity to go and collect some personal belongings. He needed to put the day in somehow and hiding out at the casino was as good as anything.

But he was nervous.

Even knowing that Jason Lee would be back in the country was making him sweat. They had been so careful to remove everything from the Villa, but what if someone Jason knew had seen them??

Amanda had told Drew not to worry. If he did find anything out, they would be long gone!

But Drew was still nervous.

Jason Lee was a big man in Newcastle; well known in Marbella. No one knew Drew in Marbella as Drew; just

Andy. But still.

And what would he do when he realised his wife and daughter and granddaughter had left?

Surely, he wouldn't just do nothing!

Would he call the police?? Would he think that they had been kidnapped?? Or worse??

The thoughts that had been building up in his head for weeks and weeks and months and months all found themselves at the forefront of his thinking as he walked towards the casino!

Drew was not just nervous he was scared.

Arriving at the casino he was greeted by his boss like an old friend. They exchanged news and Drew or Andy as his boss knew him; told him he was leaving Marbella.

Drew instinctively didn't say anymore. If Jason Lee or the police came looking for Drew at the casino; he didn't want his boss to have to lie or worse, tell them where Andy the croupier had gone. So he remained vague; he wasn't sure where he was going; just away from Marbella. He needed a change of scenery having been trapped there for the past year or so.

The lies came easily.

Drew collected his belongings; there was no reason for him to stay any longer; if need be he would just go and sit on the sea front and make the most of the afternoon sunshine before he became a man on the run with a gangster's wife, daughter and granddaughter!

Drew was nervous and scared and a little bit

LAST NOTE

apprehensive.

Without Amanda at his side; the plan seemed daft. Like a plot out of a movie!

Shouting goodbye to his old boss he was surprised when he asked Drew if he could spare a minute. He had made a phone call he said. Their casino in Tenerife was recruiting; they would snap up a good croupier like Andy! It could be the change of scenery he was looking for! The job was his if he wanted it.

Drew couldn't think straight.

He begged a couple of hours off his old boss; he told him would be back. Drew left the casino and made for the seafront just as he planned.

It was a life line; did he need a life line?? Did he not want a future with Amanda and his daughters??

Instead of sitting on the sea front he walked. He walked and he walked and he walked.

Amanda rang, It was time!

Drew Harrison knew what he had to do!

A few hours later he texts Amanda!

Amanda I love you and my daughters with all of my heart. The past months have been the happiest of my life. But I cannot run away with you. Jason will never stop looking for us. He will kill me. He will probably kill you. We can't risk it. I know I am a coward. You are the best thing that has ever happened to me. Don't look for me because I won't be there. I am at the airport about to board a flight. I'm sorry about the money. Look after my girls and yourself. I luv u

He took the sim card out of his phone and threw it into a bin.

There was no way she could contact him.

Drew had walked and walked all afternoon.

When he found himself back at the casino he knew what he had to do. His old boss had made the call; the Tenerife casino would expect him the following day; they would help him find somewhere to live. There was a flight to Tenerife later that night.

Drew Harrison had a stash of money in his pocket; there was at least 5000 euros there; more than enough to get him through until he got paid. More than enough for a flight to Tenerife.

Leaving with Amanda was too much of a risk. He was nervous and he was scared and as much as he loved them all; it was risking all of their lives; including his daughters.

Amanda would be fine. She was a survivor. He had the feeling that she would somehow make it all work with Jason. The money would help.

But there would be no more reconciliations.

If fate stepped in and they met again; Drew had the feeling that Amanda Lee would actually shoot him herself.

But realistically the chances were slim.

And then there was the added bonus that if the Lee family were all firmly planted in Marbella; he may be able to go home to Newcastle at some point; see his mam and dad and maybe even stay there if the coast was clear.

Making his way to the terminal for his flight to Tenerife; Drew heard that Jet 2 Flight LS749 from Newcastle had landed.

Jason Lee would be on that flight.

Any doubts that he was doing the wrong thing vanished. A life being chased by Jason Lee was not very appealing at all. Not for him or Amanda and certainly not for January and Maddie.

Handing over his ticket to the air stewardess she smiled at him. Drew of old noticed what a looker she was. 'Hope to see you in Playa las Americas sir!'

Drew Harrison had once again taken the money and ran. There was nothing like £10 note HE75 229564 amongst the money in his pockets; just euros. But somehow it was looking like it was going to be the same outcome!!

'Running Away Will Never Make You Free!'
Kenny Logins

15

Creative Accounting

As much as Lorna Smith didn't care about money; she probably could have told you the serial number of £10 note HE75 229564 herself.

At that time anyway. She didn't get many of them.

Lorna Smith had been a bankrupt.

Not her doing. Lorna had just paid for the consequences of her husband Neil's bad judgement.

It had made no odds to her. Money meant little. There had been much bigger losses than her bank account and up until quite recently before that; her affluence.

When Neil was 35 years old; he had walked out of the home he had shared with Lorna for 15 years; he walked into the woods; climbed a tree and killed himself. It was that simple.

At 35 years old; Lorna Smith was not only a widow; but had lost her best friend come lover come soul mate.

For a long time Lorna had just wanted to die too.

Lorna probably would have done the deed too; maybe not by hanging by a rope from a tree; but there were other methods. Lorna had thought of them all. But her mum and dad and sister Andrea never let her be. Not for a long, long time.

Not until they knew that the nonsense she had felt when Neil left her had passed and where there had been angst and hurt was just some sort of peace.

It had taken time. Lorna had suffered some sort of breakdown years earlier when any hope that she had of having children with Neil were taken away from her. Her family doubted that she had fully recovered from that blow when Neil did what he did.

Losing Neil would have been enough on its own. He had been the love of her life; the only man she had ever known. Meeting as teenagers; they sort of grew up together. In the beginning they had been more like pen pals. They met on Lorna's mum and dad's caravan site in Berwick. Neil and his family had gone for a holiday; Neil was painfully shy and a little awkward around Lorna and her overzealous younger sister Andrea. But they had exchanged addresses and then began their slow courtship.

It worked for them though; they married and set off on their marital journey living in Newcastle. Neil was an accountant; he worked at his dad's firm and for the first few years they lived in wedded bliss. Both waited in anticipation for the sound of pitter patter feet.

While they waited they travelled the world; holidaying was their greatest joy. The places they had travelled to. But still there was no sign of the stork; the one that would make their lives complete.

Test, test and more tests. Nothing wrong with Neil; it was Lorna.

All Neil could do was stand by and watch as his wife tail spinned; grieved for the babies that would never come; for the woman she would never be and even when he talked of alternatives she wouldn't listen.

She went home to her mum and dad's; Neil could do better than be with a barren woman.

But of course, Neil didn't want anyone else. He just wanted Lorna; with or without a baby.

It had taken months and months of cajoling and visits to Sunny View Caravan park to convince his wife he was happy and certainly didn't want anyone else.

They had a good life. Neil's dad retired from the business and Neil stepped up. Lorna got herself a little cleaning job at the local Primary School. Neil thought she was punishing herself; but she loved her job and loved seeing the little ones leaving school for the day.

The little income she got was Lorna's first bit of independence since she got pocket money as a kid cleaning the caravans. Not that she had ever minded not working; she would clean their house; cook meals for Neil coming in from work and of course wait for the baby.

But with no baby ever coming her days seemed different; empty. Working a couple of hours a day at the school gave her purpose.

Lorna saved her wages and when they booked their next holiday; Lorna paid for it. It was her little treat.

Running the accountancy business was beginning to take its toll on Neil though. His normal pristine time keeping was becoming erratic. Every night it got later and later. If he did bring work home he would be ferreting away in his home office until the early hours. Back up and out to work at the crack of dawn.

Lorna was worried. Neil assured her that he was fine. He had hooked a big fish he said; the first since his dad had retired. But the big fish was big with demands and Neil was working on his account flat out.

The accounts year end passed and she got Neil back. For a little while anyway.

When the police came and arrested Neil for embezzlement everything changed for ever. There had been no denying what he had been doing for Charlie Bainbridge. Neil Smith pleaded guilty, and Charlie Bainbridge pleaded not guilty. Neil was going to get the blame for everything; after all he had been getting handsomely paid for his trouble.

Everything vanished before their eyes.

The accountancy firm that Raymond Smith had built up closed virtually overnight. The house would have to be sold; there was no area of their lives that would not be slipping out of their grasp.

Neil was a shadow of who he had been. Bailed by his dad; all he could do was meet with solicitors and wait for the trial to begin. Worse case he could be sent to prison for years; best case maybe a couple of years with probation. They could survive that; just like Lorna was confident they could survive the whispers and finger pointing.

It hadn't been enough though and Neil had killed himself.

Lorna lost Neil, the house, every penny she had to her name. But it made no difference. Aside from Neil she cared little. The house they purchased when they married was bought to be a family home; Lorna didn't even have a husband never mind a family.

Her grief knew no bounds.

When her mum bundled her desperate daughter into her car and took her to Sunny View Caravan Park; Lorna had no fight left in her not to go.

The house went and the furniture and all their belongings into storage.

But the fog eventually cleared and it was time for Lorna to live some type of existence.

Penniless; the only things she had of any value was the things in storage; things that she sold. Anything she didn't went with her to the tiny one-bedroom cottage that Neil's dad had helped her to find.

And there she stayed. It was a very solitary existence in the beginning. With no bank account and with the notion in her head that no one would employ her because of what had happened; she took upon the only job that was on offer. Door to door make-up seller. It could not have been more out of her comfort zone; she barely wore make-up.

But Nikki who would be her manager was encouraging and with few other prospects on the horizon; that was what she did. She sold make-up door to door and she got her first new friend Nikki.

Nikki was the first of a handful of friends Lorna made. A handful of friends was more than she had ever had in her life. They took her out of herself; like going to York for her 40th birthday; it had just been for the day but she had loved every minute of it; she had never had a girly day out before. It had always just been her and Neil.

Madam Zita had been her friends' idea too; they paid for it.

Lorna had little time for them; it was something that she didn't take seriously. She had no faith in anything; God, spirits, Angels. But they had made it their treat and she didn't like to upset people so went along.

Madame Zita changed Lorna's life.

Lorna had gone along to her friend's house; it was a Clairvoyant Party allegedly. Lorna had been expecting Gypsy Rose Lee; she hadn't expected her to look; well normal. But Lorna sat in front of her and while she shuffled the cards that Madame Zita had given her; and she was literally blown away.

Yes she had often felt a hand touching her back. No, she didn't know about twin souls? Twin souls would always meet again?? There was no way that the woman sitting across the little table from her could have known these things; how Lorna felt and about her not being able to have babies.

It was the strangest thing though. Knowing that sometime and somewhere in the future; her soul would meet Neil's again gave Lorna some comfort. Madame Zita said it may not even be in this lifetime or the next or even the one after; but it would happen. It gave Lorna peace; the most peace she had felt in a very long time.

That and that Neil was with her; the touch of the hand on the back!! She had felt that many times. When she thought about it, it was a thing that Neil did; if he opened a door for her he would touch her back to usher her through; if they were standing in a queue, he would touch the small of her back. He hadn't left her; not completely.

With that and the arrival of her 40th birthday; Lorna decided that it was time that she went home.

There would be plenty for her to do at the caravan park; her mum and dad were a victim of their own success and the site was thriving. But they weren't getting any younger and added to that they spent their days worrying about their eldest daughter and her state of mind; seemed like the decent thing to do.

Lorna had thought that she needed to be close to where Neil was laid to rest; she didn't need to be; he walked with her. He could walk with her just as well in Berwick as he did in Newcastle.

Aside from her friends, there was nothing to keep her there for. Her friends she could keep; she had got herself a husband through her letter writing; she was sure with all the modern-day technology she could keep the contact up; she had a lot to be grateful to them for; but once she had made the decision; it was full steam ahead.

Moving back into her childhood bedroom had been a bit of a surreal experience. But when she thought about it; it was no different to any other time she had gone home. How strange had it been for her when Neil stayed there with her and they would have some fun time under the duvet. The memory made Lorna smile.

Going back to Berwick had been the right thing to do. There were so many memories that made her smile; it was the place she had met Neil!

There was always something to do. Lorna picked up the slack and then added more. It was exhausting; but she slept soundly and for the first time in a very long time; she began to feel content. She had her mum and dad; her sister Andrea lived a stones throw away with her family. Andrea's two boys had always been a joy to Lorna and Neil; it was nice being around them and getting to know the youngsters better.

Her mum and dad were right; the site was thriving.

Lorna actually loved it. The hustle and bustle was a far cry from the staidness of the one bed-roomed cottage she had lived in. Much to her own surprise she was better with people than she could have ever imagined.

She would listen to what they liked; what people thought could improve or what was missing.

Without an abundance of technical knowhow, she learned. Lorna made the Sunny View Caravan Park a Facebook, Twitter and Instagram account. She would update snippets of the site daily; got savvy on selling unexpected cancellations at short notice and very soon there were people travelling to the site from all over the country. Demand was high.

When her mum showed her the accounts from when she had arrived back in Berwick she was staggered. Lorna was making a difference.

Lorna had a purpose and it made her want to do more.

They needed a website with a booking system. As it stood it was still telephone bookings only; her mum and dad didn't even like emails; but times were changing and people liked to book everything with the touch of a button.

The website became a worry and a project for another day.

The Covid-10 Pandemic arrived, and overnight Sunny View Caravan became a ghost town. The people who were staying there had to leave and the ones that were due to book in couldn't come.

The whole situation was a conundrum.

There was only the three of them living at the site; something that her mum and dad could never recall ever happening; even in the winter the caravans were let out. But there they were; week after week cancelling the bookings and waiting for some sort of official announcement about what was going to happen.

The weather was kind though and Lorna spent her days firstly spring cleaning the caravans; then tending the outside areas; painting decking; replacing broken items; all the time under the supervision of her mum and dad, who didn't really need to supervise, but had nothing else to do.

It was the strangest of times.

Lorna's Newcastle friends set up a Zoom group, a couple of times a week they would all sit around their laptops; drink wine and discuss how they had ended up in this situation. They talked about taking a holiday abroad when they could; it seemed ironic because when they could; they didn't. Now that they couldn't it seemed like the best idea that they had ever had and couldn't wait to get booked.

The Lockdown went on for weeks and weeks; restrictions were going to be lifted; but it was going to be a phased return; the only chink of sunlight was that there was lumps of money available. Lorna's mum and dad wanted to keep it in the bank. Lorna wanted to expand the business.

The news was all about there being no travel abroad. It was all talk of 'staycations!' Holiday in England, or in their case The Borders. There was money to be made; Lorna could see that all she had to do was convince her mum and dad that whatever money they had been given would be made back and some.

And the people would come. Lorna knew that. She had felt the hand on the back when she spoke to her mum and dad about it. About maybe taking one of the other fields and developing it before the summer season began. Neil was telling her to push on; be brave. All of the things she had never been.

They walked the field that Lorna had earmarked. Then they walked it again and each time her mum and dad grew a little more animated about the prospect.

Lorna's dad checked; they already had permission for all of their land to be used for hospitality.

It was game on.

There was no way they would be able to source caravans. Staycations had sent everyone out on a mission to buy caravans; tents and the like in readiness for the summer months. Prices were through the roof.

But they could have gites.

The builder who helped with the hard standings and deckings for the caravans was called. Yes he was working and of course he was interested in doing some work for them.

Within 8 weeks there were 20 little gites in the land that used to be known as the potato field.

Each gite was fully equipped; came in 3 sizes and had running water, electricity and an outside area with a barbecue and deckchairs.

And Sunny View Caravan Park had a website with a booking system. People could book their holiday with just one click.

By the time they were ready to take bookings; all the

social media had been scrolling Sunny View Caravan Park and its development for weeks. People were following and commenting, sharing with friends. The Government said yes; Lorna set the website live and they were fully booked for the rest of the year within 48 hours.

Lorna Smith was so pleased with herself.

It was the busiest summer season they had ever had.

When Lorna's Newcastle friends came to stay in one of the gites for a long weekend; they were blown away with everything that Lorna had achieved. And for once, Lorna took the weekend off; stayed in the gites with her friends and behaved like a tourist. They drank and ate and sat outside and all agreed that none of them needed the Costa Blanca when they had a friend with a caravan site.

Despite all of the restrictions with Lockdown, despite everything that had gone on before she had come home; Lorna had done the right thing. She had found her place.

Obviously the 5 star reviews that appeared on their website was a plus too.

And the proof was in the pudding.

When Lorna released the booking system for the following year; it was same again. Sold out in no time.

True; there was still talk of Staycations and no doubt they would have some cancellations if restrictions were lifted for overseas holidays; but still. For every cancellation there would be someone waiting in the wings for one of their caravans or gites.

Lorna had really shown her salt during the pandemic. She had seen the opportunity; used the funds wisely and it had resulted in a thriving business. A business that slowly, slowly began to be more and more of Lorna's responsibility.

Lorna loved it.

Keeping busy was helping her heal. Neil was a constant; she often felt like he was her biggest cheerleader, but rather than make her sad; it made her smile. The grief would sometimes come and wash over her; but then someone would need a gas bottle changing or something and she didn't get chance to wallow.

Sea View Caravan Site is still a thriving business nowadays.

It is all overseen by its manager; Lorna Smith.

Lorna Smith who once knew that £10 note HE75 229564 had been in her possession; she had that little.

Nowadays she still barely sees any cash; everything is paid directly into the bank when customers make their bookings. Even anything that is purchased on site is paid for using a little debit style card that customer buy on the Sea View Caravan site website; they are the currency for their holidays.

It was a savvy business move by Lorna. The cards could be loaded in £10 increments; many over loaded, but never redeemed. It was money in the bank for Lorna. She had come a long way since the time she was buying train tickets for her and her Newcastle friends to go to York to celebrate her 40th birthday. When the £10 note HE75 229564 made a difference to her life; she was so on the breadline.

Her life in Newcastle felt like it happened to someone else. If she thought about it, it felt like it was like recapping a movie she had seen. Young girl falls in love; gets married, lives an idyllic life; husband steals, husband dies, wife lives in poverty. The End.

But it hadn't been the end. In some ways it was a just the beginning. There was no man; that was something she wasn't ready for; Neil had been everything to her and was a hard act to follow. But she would never say never.

In her mid-forties meeting Mr Right or almost Right was not on her radar. The chances of her meeting another Mr Right was slim though. Work kept her busy. She had her Newcastle friends who she had just booked her first holiday abroad with; it had taken that long! She had Berwick friends; mainly people who worked at the caravan site; but friends came from everywhere and she loved it when they all went out for a curry or to the theatre together.

It was the little things.

It hadn't been the life that Lorna Smith had envisaged when she made that first train journey to Newcastle to meet Neil thought as she sat at her little desk working on a spreadsheet.

The crunch of car on the gravel outside sounded the arrival of guest.

LAST NOTE

Lorna stood ready to go and check the arrivals in.

She could feel the pressure on the small of her back. Neil pushing her towards the door ....

'Tis Better to Have Loved and Lost Than to Have Never Loved at All.'

Alfred Lord Tennyson

16

They Know the Cost of Everything and the Value of Nothing!

Jackie Newall was one of Lorna Smith's Newcastle friends.

One day Lorna had knocked on Jackie's door and timidly tried to sell her make-up.

Lorna didn't know Jackie; but Jackie knew Lorna. She had remembered her from when she was a cleaner at her kids primary school and later from news articles when Lorna's husbands demise and death were out there for the world to see.

Jackie took pity on Lorna and her door to door make up business; placed an order and that was the beginning of their friendship. Jackie would always insist that Lorna stayed for a coffee when she brought her delivery and they sort of jelled.

Lorna Smith was really nice and over the years Jackie took her advice on many occasions when her job as a councillor demanded a second opinion or just a confidant for that matter. Lorna wasn't a tittle tattle and on many occasions; Jackie would find herself ringing her friend and asking her to point her in the right direction.

Despite everything that had happened to Lorna; she had empathy for people.

Anyway Lorna had handed £10 note HE75 229564 in change that she had got when she paid for her latest toiletries that Lorna had sold her.

Jackie's husband, Jack thought she was mad for keep putting orders in; surely Lorna Smith knew that there was no way on earth a family of four could get through all the bottles bubble bath, shower gel and shampoo that kept arriving on a regular basis on their doorstep.

But Jackie didn't mind.

Years later; when Lorna Smith had returned to her home town and no deliveries of bubble bath, shower gel and shampoo arrived; Jack was grateful for the stockpile in the bottom of his wife's wardrobe.

Jackie Newall was the local councillor; had been for a decade and if it wasn't blowing her own trumpet too much; was dammed good at it. She was a doer and her doing attitude had made a difference over the years.

Jackie was proud of her achievements.

Not everything she set out to do had the ending she would have hoped for; but just having a go gave her respect throughout her ward; that and her door always open policy.

The open door policy had been a bit of a problem in the beginning. When Jackie had first been elected to councillor; she had no idea that so many people had so many issues. Jack had happily allowed his wife to convert one of their front rooms into her office and even when she had advertised that he would be having a 'surgery' at home one day a week; she truly did not think that it would entail an ever evolving door.

One day a week became two and even though Jack and the kids were forever up and down answering the door; making cups of tea and having small talk with strangers who sat in their hallway waiting their turn, they just got on with it.

Jackie's family had been her biggest cheerleaders when she had decided to stand to be a councillor in the first place. They could hardly complain.

Over the years they all got used to the madness though.

They got used to Jackie's latest passion for getting something done and would help where they could.

Jackie Newall was getting herself a name for taking on the big boys and if not winning; then making them at least think about the consequences of their actions.

The women's refuge!

Help for homeless!

Council housing!

Then there were the million and one other things she did that sometimes just stayed under the radar.

For a being a councillor not being a job; it was full on.

But Jackie loved it. She liked to think she was making a difference.

It wasn't always easy having a home life and being very much in demand from the public.

There were a few months when the family needed her more than ever. First Jack's mam died. Jack's dad who had never had to look after himself for a single day in his married life couldn't cope so Jackie and Jack made the decision to bring him to live with them.

What started off fine for the first few months became even more of a challenge when he seemed to deteriorate almost overnight. It had been hard to watch and even harder to handle him.

It was very apparent that he needed better care than they could give him; even the stairs to his room were becoming too much for him. He seemed to have forgotten how to use his legs and needed one of them to push each leg on to the step-in front. Every time was a slow process; one that Jack's dad scream with as if in pain, but the doctor assured them that his legs were working fine; it was just his state of mind.

In the midst of all of that, Jackie's dad died. It was unexpected. He'd had angina for years but had managed it well; then one day while he was getting his car washed, it had been lights out.

So six months after Jack's mam had died; Jackie's dad had.

This time Jackie knew it would be her mam that would need help. Jackie had her dad's 'can do' attitude. Unfortunately, Jackie's mam's mentality was that she 'can't do it!'

Without a shadow of a doubt, Jackie's mam was going to need residential care.

So Jackie found herself having to see if she could pull some favours in.

Two residential places were needed as soon as possible.

Luckily it wasn't so much the favours were found. It was the timing of her search. There was one room available at one end of town and another at the other. They were lucky.

But they had no sooner got Jackie's mam into her room and Jack's dad into the room at his specialist home than Covid-19 came and it was going to be quite some time before Jackie and Jack saw their parents again. At least not seeing them through a window.

Both Jackie and Jack were riddled with guilt. If only they had tried for a little longer to help Jack's dad. They could have made some room for him on the lower floor of their house; they had the office and the dining room; one of them could easily have been converted into a bedroom for Jack's dad.

Maybe both rooms could have and Jackie's mam could have come to stay too.

For some time the Newells' were laden with guilt. But how were they to know that there would be a National Lockdown. That care homes were going to have to close their doors for months so that the pesky virus couldn't attack the most vulnerable in the community.

Jackie called both homes every day. They even tried a few Facetime calls; but that confused Jack's dad and Jackie's mam just wasn't interested; she wouldn't even talk to her daughter on the phone. Jackie and Jack had to rely on the kindness of the staff to keep them updated.

Becka came back from university at the first stirrings of their being a lockdown. Dean who had been virtually living at his girlfriend Sara's parents' house for years came back too. With Sara on tow.

To be honest Jackie did think that Sara and Dean were being sensible; Sara's parents' house was small; it made sense for them to come and camp out at the 3 storey Victorian house that Dean had been brought up in.

Overnight; Jackie's home seemed to lose one resident with the departure of Jack's dad to the care home and the arrival of Beck; Dean and Sara.

It made things easier for Jack and Jackie; there wasn't time to think their parents in their respective care homes; it was a bit of a blessing in disguise.

It was the strangest of times.

There were no surgeries so the front doorbell stopped ringing.

Everyone was unsure what was happening. It felt like every day was a Bank Holiday without the pub or a trip to the Metrocentre.

Jackie and Jack took walks. Lots of them. Jackie made scrumptious food for the family; even digging out her old Bero book from when the kids were little and make pies; scones and cakes. It was just as well they were doing so much walking or she would have ended up the like a little barrel.

But the novelty of endless days of Bank Holidays soon wore off and Jackie decided that maybe she should see how her constituents were doing.

Facebook became her greatest communication tool.

People raised their concerns; there were all sorts of things; people living on their own who were scared to go to the shops; dog poo; covid testing kits; people living on the streets with no support; lack of children's schooling and hidden amongst it all was domestic violence.

Jackie hadn't thought about how people were fairing in lockdown relationship wise. Her own home was a happy one; there had been a few hard words between Becka and Dean; but they were brother and sister; they had always been like that. And Sara was so quiet she hardly knew she was there.

But not everyone lived in big houses where everyone could have their own space inside and out.

Jackie fired off emails. There were some women and children in some very dangerous situations and she thought that although the extra rooms at the Women's Refuge had never been needed; she thought that they would maybe have to get them made ready.

By the end of the first lockdown; the refuge was having to divert people to another refuge. Things had got so bad.

It was the same with the homeless. It was young Kai who had raised the alert with Jackie.

Kai Logan; the young homeless boy who on a whim Jackie had handed £10 note HE75 229564 to when he was begging on the Town Hall steps. He had later befriended Jackie as she went to make her way home. Her act of kindness had made him think about his mam and he decided that he wanted to go home.

Jackie had been so happy to help the young 15-year-old boy. If one of hers had ever taken it upon themselves to run away; she would like to think that there was someone out there that would help. Jackie always thought that there were more good than bad people; but Kai hadn't seemed to meet any of the good ones in a very long time.

Kai went home to his family and Jackie got a new friend. He always kept in touch; updated Jackie on his life. She became like an auntie to him. And a fairy godmother to his mam and dad who always thanked her whenever she saw them.

Kai called and asked if anything had been done about the homeless?? With no restaurants and pubs open and with people not going to work or anything would mean that there were no scraps of food or money for the homeless to eat.

Jackie had never thought about it but promised Kai she would.

The homeless shelter had gone in to some sort of shut down; there hadn't been the staff the volunteer manager had told her. They had literally had to close their doors and step over the people who were sleeping on the steps.

Jackie hadn't meant to have a go at the manager; it wasn't as if it was their responsibility; but she did say that they should have raised the alarm before closing the doors.

Fortunately the weather was fine so sleeping rough wasn't going to be life threatening; but the lack of funds and food was. If the homeless weren't getting it given, they would simply start to steal it.

Very quickly Jackie had herself a team of volunteers; food donations and even though it was against the rules; Jackie had gone to collect Kai. If anyone knew where the homeless hung out; it was Kai.

The Refuge reopened and with all of the food donations; a team of cooks began making meals.

Within days The Refuge was a safe place where anyone could call in for a wash, a meal and some company; even if they did have to sit at a 2 metre distance apart.

The running of The Refuge was something that was ongoing until the end of the Pandemic and beyond. Just like the Women's Refuge; the need for it was relentless.

Thanks to Kai, it was a job well done.

Jackie only managed to see her mam once. Not that her mam would ever have recognised her; she was completely hidden under her protective clothing. The home had made an exception; her mam was dying and Jackie had been called in to sit with her as she made her journey off this earth.

Never having a particular close relationship with her mam; it was a peaceful and serene time. Jackie thought of her childhood and thought when it was that her mam had lost interest in her. There was nothing that she could remember; it was just the way her mam was. She had always been wrapped up in Jackie's dad; sometimes Jackie thought that her and her brother were just nuisances.

But still. It was still her mam and with her brother being stuck with him family in London and no way to be able to make the journey under the restrictions; Jackie stayed with their mam alone. She sat for three days and then her mam was gone.

A funeral during the pandemic was a strange experience. There were only 4 mourners; Jackie, Jack, Dean and Becka. The service itself was transmitted via Teams to anyone who couldn't get there. Jackie knew her brother would be watching. But hand on heart; even if the funeral had been in normal times, there wouldn't be many more mourners. Her mam wasn't a mixer.

And life continued on for the Newall family. Dean and Sara worked from home; one in their bedroom; the other in the dining room. Becka did some sort of improvised University work; Jack worked half the week and remained furloughed the rest and Jackie did whatever it was she had to do, always keeping a keen eye on both the town refuges and the other on her Bero book.

They all socialised best they could.

Beer gardens after a long walk were Jackie and Jack's favourite times; but she also loved her drinks nights with her friends; all done over the wonders of Zoom.

But slowly but surely restrictions began to lift.

Jackie did wonder if things would ever really go back to normal. As much as she hated the dusty town hall council meetings; she missed them. It just wasn't the same trying to argue her point on a Zoom call when all the time she knew she was wearing her slippers; it just didn't feel right. She felt like she had lost the power.

The whole family upped sticks and had a Staycation in the Lakes; it was very much home from home. Same routine; different location. But the weather had been good and the location views were stunning.

Jackie even managed a little girls weekend; the first she had ever had; she had only even had day trips with her friends. But a group of them had gone and stayed in one of Lorna Smith's gites.

What a dark horse Lorna had been. Timid shy Lorna Smith had given her mam and dad's caravan site a complete facelift and was making a fortune off all of the holidaymakers that weren't able to travel to foreign shores. Jackie was so impressed with the gites she thought that it would be an option for a holiday for her lot.

By the time Jack was able to see his dad; his dad had no idea who Jack was. It had been such a long time since they had seen each other. Even though Jack's dad had greeted his son warmly; he thought he was one of the carers in the home. It broke Jack. He had been often and waved to his dad through his bedroom window; his dad had always waved back. But maybe all that time he had thought that Jack worked there.

They dealt with it though.

Jackie wondered if Jack's dad would have been better if the home wasn't in its own enforced lockdown and regular visitors would have been able to go in. Perhaps not; he had forgot about his legs long before the home; the disease had already started eating in.

He survived just under another year. One day he forgot how to breathe and that was that. In less than two years Jackie and Jack had lost all of their parents.

It made them think.

With the sale of both houses, Jackie and Jack were in a good financial position. Their own mortgage only had a couple of years left. Perhaps it was time they thought about retiring themselves. Make the most of whatever time they had left.

The pandemic had made lots of people re-evaluate their lives. Work out what was important to them and what wasn't.

They thought long and hard.

As much as Jackie Newell loved being a councillor; she didn't run for the third term.

Jack gave up his work in the factory; as soon as word went out that they would be returning to full shifts he put his notice in.

LAST NOTE

They paid off the remainder of the mortgage; thought about selling the house and then changed their minds again. It was their home and even though people still knocked on the door to have a word with Jackie; it was far more seldom these days.

Jackie didn't give everything up.

There was no way she could be fully retired; she was just in her fifties for God's sake.

She became a trustee for the Women's Refuge and the Homeless Refuge. She is as passionate about them as ever; and now that she wasn't a councillor she worked even harder for them.

They bought themselves a caravan and made the most of their unexpected freedom.

One of their favourite places to go was Sunny View Caravan Park; there was always a warm welcome waiting for them off Lorna Smith and her family.

Money was not the be all and end all for Jackie Newall. She had given £10 note HE75 229564 away easily. But she knew what the value of it could be for someone else.

*'You Have Two Hands – One to Help Yourself
the Second to Help Others.'*

Anon

17

Show Me the Money!!

Kai Logan had been the person that Jackie Newall had so generously given £10 note HE75 229564 to. It hadn't been a big deal for her; she had taken one look at the desperate face of the young boy on the Town Hall steps and instead of given him the loose change she had intended giving him; she had given him the note.

For Kai it was a game changer.

No one had been that generous with him in a very long time; not since he had lived at home with his mam and dad.

When the waitress in the café that he went to with £10 note HE75 229564 undercharged him and overfed him; he knew that despite the consequences; he wanted to go home.

It had been a long time since he had run away; Kai thought maybe about six months; but time was something he didn't have any concept of anymore. He just knew when the sun rose it was the start of a new day and when it set it was the end. The bit in the middle; the dark bit was the scariest.

When he had left home he hadn't taken the thought of having all his belongings stolen off him; his phone had been the hardest. It was his only connection to home; without it everything seemed a million times worse.

As young as he was; Kai knew he had made a mistake running away.

In the darkest of nights he would lie in his sleeping bag with one eye open in case someone tried to rob him or worse and try and think of one single reason why he had left the comfort of his mam and dad's house.

There wasn't really anything; it was just that his mam and dad loved him too much.

Stupid reason to run away.

Kai had a twin brother. One night when they were babies they had gone to sleep and only Kai had woken up.

Always fearing that something would happen to their surviving son; his mam and dad had always protected Kai; when his friends played out in the streets; he would be in the garden. When his friends started venturing further afield Kai couldn't go unless either his mam and dad took him there and back.

For young Kai it had felt suffocating. He wasn't a baby anymore.

But he cried like a baby when the nice lady on the steps had said she would take him home. He cried in the car while she knocked his terrified mam and dad out of their beds and he cried when at long last his mam and dad cuddled their runaway son in their arms.

There were a lot of tears for days and days as different family members came to welcome young Kai home.

It took Kai a long time to settle back into his life at home. He had been living off his wits so long that to even be given food on a regular basis made him feel ill. His sleeping was erratic, and he couldn't sleep at all unless his bedside lamp was left on.

One night the bulb must have popped and Kai woke up to darkness. He had no idea where he was; he thought being at home had just been a dream and he was still living rough on the streets. He must have screamed because just as he thought he was going to stop breathing; his dad was there; the light from the landing illuminating his bedroom. He cried with relief; but it wasn't the last time that he had a panic attack.

For the first time; Kai and his mam and dad talked about Luke. He had always been a type of elephant in the room; no one mentioned him; there weren't even any photographs of when the twins were born. Luke's death had just been one of those things; it happened. But not talking about him had been worse than if they did. Kai would often think that maybe the wrong brother had died.

But it got better. Seeing pictures of his baby brother gave him some sort of peace he had never had before. Kai realised he had the twin thing but had no one to share it with. Putting a face to Luke made it a little less scary. They had been identical; but the baby face of Luke would always the one he would be remembered for; the face that Kai could now carry around in his heart.

Kai now had the strength of two men.

Even with his absence from school for months on end; Kai managed to get some pretty decent results; enough to get him on to an A Level course at college; very impressive results seeing as he never set foot in school again.

It was different at college though; he knew a few people, but none in any of his classes and he was old news by then and most of them would probably have forgotten about the boy who walked out of school one day and never went back.

Kai still found the whole college thing a struggle.

The noise was scary; Kai had spent quite a lot of his time as a runaway on his own. The sound of silence was something he got used to. No earphones with music playing; no mobile with constant chatter; no friends. The only sound he heard were his thoughts.

Even back at home; the television would be on low and if he was gaming whereas before he would have headphone and mic on; nowadays he just played; again with the volume down low. His normal was certainly not the normal he had before.

His school friends had all been regulars at his house since he got back; they were all different though. His mates had all gone girl mad and looked forward to a

Friday night when they would get someone to get them some drink or some form of drugs and they would all head off to the park in the hope of getting with the girl in school that they had been talking about for weeks.

Kai was different in an entirely different way. He had lived on the streets long enough to know all about drink and drugs; it held no appeal. He hadn't befriended a lot of people on his travels; but one of the two that he had spoken to seemed to have been living the nomadic lifestyle because of drink or drugs or gambling. Kai had been there once; living rough. He would always strive never to return there. So when his mates went off to the park on a Friday night; he stayed home. They never pressed him. To them too, Kai thought, he was different now too.

It was fine though. Even if he was different it was more to do that he had grown up very quickly; seen things that his school friends probably never understood and done things they would have thought Kai Logan possible of. He knew himself that he was a little aloof; a little odd even.

So making new college friends was the only fly in his college life; the work he could handle, he even liked the discipline of having a timetable to follow. It brought timekeeping and time management back into his life.

In class, little groups congregated together; some small, some bigger. Kai never tried to force his way in; if they invited then he would happily join them. But his communication skills weren't that good, he had lost interest in things that were the main topics of conversation; the music charts; movies, what people were watching on the television or where was good to go. The only thing that he seemed to carry from the past was the love of his football team.

Because he said little when he was in a group environment; the next time they were all together; they tended to forget to invite him.

Kai didn't mind. Pretending to have interest in something that held no interest for him was worse than not being invited at all.

Despite his solitary existence at college he ended up enjoying the whole experience; got A Level grades better than he ever could have hoped for and set University in his sight.

His mam and dad were so proud of him.

Still unsure what it was he wanted to do at University; for weeks on end his mam and dad accompanied him to all sorts of open days at Universities throughout the North East.

None of the mainstream courses appealed to him.

Thinking that he was maybe going to have to think of getting a job while he worked out what he wanted to do; it was his dad who gave Kai a glimmer of hope about what would hold his interest enough to enable him to complete a degree and maybe a profession in.

Kai and his dad were sitting in the garden; they had been there some time. His dad was having a beer or two and they were just sitting enjoying each other's company and putting the world to right.

Tentatively his dad asked him what it was like sleeping out under the stars every night. They had often talk about what Kai's life had been like; but Kai had always managed to generalise and change the subject. But that night; sitting outside on the warm night; it didn't seem so daunting.

Kai talked. He told his dad about the sleeping bag he had stolen; how it was his most prized possession and would hide it away from thieving hands when actual fact he had stolen it himself. He told of always sleeping with one eye open. How he got to know the noises of the night. How he knew the difference between a human footstep to that of an animal; say a fox or a deer or a rat.

He told of the nights when he couldn't sleep and would lie and look at the sky. Sometimes it would be cloudy and overcast; other nights; like that night, the skies were clear and you could see all of the stars.

Kai hadn't a clue about star or constellations or planets for that matter; but over the months he got to know the different shapes the stars made; or which stars shine brightly and where they sat in relation to the rest of the stars. He talked of the moons; full crescent, half. How the moon would appear and then different stages of not just the month; but even during the night.

The sky had been something that he had been researching when he came home. He could remember vividly what each pattern of stars looked like and would scour the internet until he found them; he had even started filling in a notebook full of stars and moons and suns and planets.

His dad offered Kai a beer; he took it, one now and again didn't hurt him. 'There's your answer Kai; that's what you need to get a degree in!'

And his dad was right. The skies had been a big part of his life as a runaway. It helped him focus; he got to know about them without knowing a thing about them.

There were no courses open to him locally; he really didn't want to think about leaving home again. But he could do courses via distance learning.

It was perfect for Kai. It would involve having to go on some courses; but they would be short residential ones; he could do that. Especially if the others on the course would have the same interests as him and not about pop culture or what pub in Newcastle did 10 shots for £7 quid.

The Covid-19 pandemic made little difference to Kai Logan's life.

All his studies were done in the walls of his home; the only resources he needed was a laptop and internet connection. Everything he needed was at his fingertips.

The course work had been set out at the beginning of the University year; there were no live online lectures; but there was a vast library of lectures from previous years and with little else to do; Kai made the most of them.

Even with his mam and dad being home all of the time; they both had jobs in hospitality; his mam was a receptionist at a big city centre hotel and his dad was the handyman at the same hotel so they had months and months of being furloughed, they just let Kai get on with whatever it was he was doing.

He did walk a lot with them though.

They would even pack up a picnic and head off in whatever direction they fancied. Their little town was surrounded by countryside so there was always somewhere to go; places that they had never been to even though they had lived there longer than Kai had been born. They would walk and walk; Kai marvelled at everything around him; being a runaway had made him think so much more about his environment that he had done before he left.

It made him think though. What if he had still been living rough when this pandemic hit. What if there were no bins full of scraps or people walking to and from work willing to throw a forlorn looking Kai a quid or two.

Kai couldn't think of what would have happened to him. There was a refuge in town but surely it would be full to the rafters.

On a whim he rang Jackie Newell, the lady who had kindly given him £10 note HE75 229564 which had changed his life and took him home.

They had kept in touch. Jackie had been so worried about him the night she dropped him off in the safety of his mam and dad. He knew himself that he had been a sight for sore eyes; skin and bone and a complete wreck emotionally.

She had kept up contact and even called to see him if she was passing.

Jackie Newell had no idea what was happening with The Refuge. Or the plight of the homeless, but she promised she would make it her business.

And she had been as good as her word. The Refuge had closed; but she had it reopened. Kai had the utmost respect for Jackie Newell, she certainly got things done. She had even came and picked him up so he could help get the word out to people living on the streets; after all he knew where most of them would be.

It was an eye opener for Kai. He had memories of his time living rough; some he would rather forget and others; like the skies, were more whimsical these days. Coping mechanism.

What shocked Kai most was how they all looked so hopeless. He almost asked Jackie if he had looked like that too. He didn't he didn't need to know; he knew how he had felt.

His good deed probably ended up being his misfortune. He hadn't been anywhere else for the whole of lockdown; just with his mam and dad and even if they met people on their walk; they all stayed apart. Even his nan had given them all a wide berth when they called to see them; they weren't allowed past the gate. So when Kai caught the covid virus; the only place he could have come into contact with anyone that was likely to be infected was his day out with the homeless people and in the Refuge.

LAST NOTE

Boy was he ill. He could barely lift his head for weeks; his mam and dad would come into his room wearing masks and gloves; he had no appetite. He had a raging temperature; his chest felt like it was on fire and sometimes when he coughed he thought he was going to choke.

His mam spoke to the doctor; his chest and immune system would have been compromised when he was sleeping rough; but he was young and fit so rather than admit him into hospital; they were riding it out at home.

At some points he would hallucinate; there would be homeless people in his room; not like the ones he had met when he had been homeless himself; these were grotesque figures who would be in his room; sit on his bed; touch his face and try and kiss him. He was terrified; he would wake up screaming and sweating. His mam and dad would be there; freakishly masked up and assuring him everything was going to be okay!

Slowly he recovered; again!

For a long time, he felt as weak as a kitten. All he could manage to do was make it downstairs and maybe sit in the garden. His eating improved and so did his strength; though the raking cough was a constant; it just wouldn't shift. No one knew enough about the damage that the virus left you with; the cough, the doctor said, would go in its own time.

It did, eventually. Thanks to a million and one spoon full of honey that his nan had insisted he took every day.

Kai resumed his studies. The lecturers were back on line and his university life went on very much like pre-covid days. But there was to be no residential courses; not on his course anyway; it would just be too difficult to arrange. Apart from that; Kai returned his assignments on time and was pleased when his predicted degree was deemed to be a 1st with Honours.

His mam and dad returned to their day jobs; the hotel reopened and Kai found himself alone in the house for the first time in a very long time.

Every day he took walks; some routes he had walked with his mam and dad; other days he found his own way. It made Kai feel content being out in the wide open spaces with the trees and animals. His degree was finished; he just had to work out what to do with it. Being outdoors helped him focus his mind.

For Kai, it felt ironic. He loved being in the house; he had no social life to speak of, he didn't mind. He still kept in touch with his friends, but they had jobs and girlfriends and it was only through texts and social media that he kept in touch with them all. Kai had no desire to go meet them in a pub. None of the things that he should be doing appealed to him.

He liked going on his walks. He liked to look at the skies at night. Beyond that; he was happy to stay home; research things that interested him and of course watch football; he even thought that he would like to go and play again; but that would depend on his health.

The cough had gone; but his chest was still weak. A

legacy of the Covid or had the damage been done when he had ran away?

Kai was an enigma to himself.

He had friends who were girls; mainly ones he had gone to school with, but there were a couple on his degree course who he had struck up a type of friendship with. He had no desire to have a relationship with a girl, not a boyfriend/girlfriend type of relationship. There just wasn't the want or the need.

Kai thought that maybe he was gay. As Kai did he did some research on his laptop. Three or four porn movies later; it did nothing for him. So not gay either!

He was nothing; neither straight or gay. It just didn't interest him. Was it another legacy from when he had run away?

When he had first gone, he had lived in a squat. He hadn't been there very long really; but he had seen and heard enough. There were girls selling their bodies; boys selling their bodies. Other residents sharing their bodies with each other. Kai had never been involved; never been asked to be. But he had seen lots. It had made him feel ill.

Even though he had known about the birds and the bees for a long time before he left home and had even seen things on the internet. Nothing could have prepared him for people having sex with each other in front of him.

Maybe his disinterest stemmed from there.

Maybe he was traumatised.

Or was it the fact that he never really went anywhere to meet anyone.

But Kai Logan wasn't unhappy. Far from it. He had the world at his feet. He just had to decide what he wanted to do.

He had gone and got himself a First Degree with Honours in Astronomy.

His mam and dad could not have been prouder, he was proud.

The environment and climate control was an area he thought he might like to work in. If there was something he'd had experience in more than the moon and the stars; it was the world around them.

£10 note HE75 229564 was a life saver for Kai. By being given the £10 note as a kind gesture it opened up Kai Logan's eyes. That maybe he could get himself off the streets and get home.

Home to his family.

Home to an opportunity of a life that would make a difference.

Kai Logan had lived a life that none of us could imagine. A life in the elements living on his wits. All before he was 16 years old. £10 note HE75 229564 had been his meal ticket home!

'Being Homeless is Like Living in a Post-Apocalyptic World. You're on the Outskirts of Society!'

Frank Dillane

18

Cross My Palm

Emma Keep was Emma Keeps when she gained possession of £10 note HE75 229564.

Not much of a difference; but for Emma they were a million miles apart.

Emma had been working in a café when the door had opened and Kai Logan had come in. As he ordered food; Emma had taken a good long look at him. He was far too young to be living on the streets; he looked like an urchin. Dirty faced; dirty clothes and a total look of despondency all over him. Emma's heart went out to him. What could possibly had happened to him for him to end up in the state he was.

Kai had handed over £10 note HE75 229564 to Emma and if he had been a little less hungry and a little more alert; he would have noticed that she had given him almost £10 back in change for the food he had ordered.

Handing over a pudding he hadn't ordered; Emma could hear how well spoken and polite he was. You would have thought she had given him a golden goose.

Locking up later Emma hoped beyond hope that

somehow the boy would find his way home; or at to somewhere that wasn't living on the streets; especially on a night like it was that night. It was so cold.

Emma counted her blessings. She maybe wasn't living the life she thought she would be. Somehow she had thought by now she would have been discovered; would be living her dream as an actress. But at 25 she was still living at home with her mam; made ends meet working two jobs; the first in the café she had just locked up; the other as barmaid in a city centre club.

And all the while she waited for her 'big break' that hadn't materialised.

Emma had been given hope. But that had been weeks earlier and the only saving grace that she had was that she hadn't told anyone so hadn't been left with egg on her face. She had been so sure so had got the part; well not sure just a feeling that she had been what they were looking for.

But she had been kidding herself. It was one of, if not the biggest continued serial on British television; why would they be interested in Emma Keeps from Newcastle. It had made the usual up tempo Emma feel a bit down on her heels.

Then came Madame Zita; her mam had booked her for a drinks night with her friends; Emma had forgotten all about it. But as each of her mam's friends had filed out of the living room; being quite frankly; amazed. Emma took the chance and added herself onto the end of the queue.

Emma took a seat in front of Madame Zita when her turn came. She looked nothing like what Emma had envisaged her; she looked normal.

Crossing her palm with Emma well-earned £15; including £10 note HE75 229564; Emma waited patiently to be amazed.

If ever there was an understatement; then being amazed was that. Emma was blown away.

There was no way Madame Zita could have known what she knew. She didn't know Emma from Adam. Even if she had seen Emma in one of the local productions; she couldn't have known that she had been for an audition in London for a role that would change her life forever.

She had though. She had told Emma that she could see her surrounded by stars. That's she would get the recognition and reward that she desired. No matter how long it took.

The weeks past and there was still no news from London. Emma began to think that Madame Zita was just hocus pocus. What could she know anyway?? All Emma could do was wait for the reject letter and think about her life going forward. The café and club weren't proper jobs; they had only ever been fill in's while she waited to be discovered. But if she wasn't going to be an actress she really needed to find a proper job.

And somewhere to live. She couldn't stay at her mam's forever.

When Paul, her agent called to tell her the news; she

didn't take in a word he said. All she managed to utter was 'email me the details!'

Travelling to London, Emma read and re-read the email a thousand times.

Emma had got the part. Just as Madame Zita had predicted.

Emma Keep was born.

It was only ever going to be for 8 episodes; all top secret because of the explosive story live and the arrival of Emma Keep as Valentine Mitchell.

Valentine Mitchell and Emma Keep got such a great reception off the watching audience that she stayed for two years.

Emma would pinch herself every morning. She was living in London; had become a household name virtually overnight. She mixed with stars of stage and screen and when she met a young footballer called Luke Chambers; she was fit to burst.

Like her, Luke hailed from the North East. That was how they had initially started talking. They were at the same 'do' and when Emma ordered herself a drink from the bar; Luke had asked her if she was from Newcastle.

He had no idea who she was, and she had no idea who he was. They chatted for ages before someone came and asked for an autograph; Luke thought it was for him, after all he played for one of the biggest clubs in London; but it had been Emma Keep's signature they wanted.

It was a relationship built on where they came from

rather than who they were.

They were just like any other young couple. Behind closed doors anyway. In public there was always a camera being pushed in their faces or someone wanting a selfie taken with them or an autograph. They were a hot topic couple.

As Emma's contract was nearing its end; a North East director had got in touch and offered her the part of Cushie Butterfield. Emma was intrigued.

When she was little her Nan used to sing her the little ditty that was local folklore; Cushie Butterfield. Emma had always loved it. And she loved the role she had been offered.

It was the story of a young girl who won the pools. She was handed the publicity cheque to her by a rich businessman who was twice her age. They fell in love and after a messy divorce from his first wife, they married. The drama would portray her life, her relationship with her step-children, her affairs, drugs and alcohol dependency, her husband's death and her falling hopelessly in love with a local footballer and their life together.

Art mimicking life?? Maybe. But it was to be a 6 part drama; all set in the North East.

For Emma Keep it was a no brainer. Her contract was almost up, but to utter astonishment the producers told her they would leave the door open. Emma could go off and do her own thing and then if she wanted to; she could go back.

She was a lucky young lady.

This time when she went home, she rented a house. Her mam was now living with her boyfriend; the first decent one she'd had in a very long time. Emma didn't want to intrude; more so when Luke came up; there would be too much interest in them.

So she had found a little house; far enough out of the way not to draw attention to the comings and goings and set about learning her part.

It was the best four months Emma had ever had.

She took on the role with ease; playing a role from young to old was something she had never had to do before; but she loved it.

Luke would come and stay when he could. And it was lovely to have their families all meet up at their house.

Emma could have stayed there forever.

But filming ended and it was time to pack up the house and return to London. There would be lots of publicity to do for Cushie Butterfield.

Emma Keep's role as Cushie Butterfield turned out to be her first Bafta nomination. It had been so well received. She didn't win; but being nominated for it had been enough; the list of fellow nominees was full of established drama actresses; Emma came from soap so it was quite a feat.

Emma couldn't settle back in London.

She did think about knocking on the door of the soap and asking them to retrieve her part; maybe she was unsettled because she wasn't really doing anything. Most days she would just be in the flat; Luke would be at training or at matches and she was left to her own devices.

Every day she scoured the housing market at home. Luke had agreed; even if they didn't live there, at some point they would want to put down roots. Eventually she found something; not far from where she had rented a house the year before. Without them even seeing it; Luke and Emma bought it; there first big commitment.

All the talk was of the UK going into some sort of lockdown. Emma could not bear the thought of being stuck in London; so as soon as the sale went through on their house, Emma made her way North.

Buying blind had been a bit of a risk; but as soon as she set foot in the front door Emma loved it. It needed work, but it was liveable; which was just as well because a week later Lockdown became a reality and unexpectedly, Luke came home too. There was going to be no football for the foreseeable.

And so Emma and Luke lived in their new house in the North East.

They didn't have a lot of furniture; they didn't have time to get any. But they would make do; they had all of the essentials though.

Their days were mainly spent in the garden; usually kicking a football about and their nights were spent snuggled up on the only sofa they had in the living room; a 2 seater that Luke's dad had dropped them off.

They watched the news avidly.

So many people were doing random things and all of a sudden; Emma and Luke found themselves using Tik Toc and making little videos of themselves. It didn't matter what they did; cooking, playing football, singing daft songs; everything was video'd and posted on line.

People loved them.

Emma and Luke were still popular. Their following grew by the thousands every day.

More than that; it was keeping them sane.

They saw almost no one.

If anything was going to test their relationship; isolation was.

But they coped. When it was deemed that football can be played again; Luke went back off to London to train.

Restrictions had lifted and Emma could go and see her mam and John; she could be in their bubble. But it was a lonely time. There was no indication when the 'arts' would be able to resume again. Until then, Emma never read every script that landed in her email box; usually she would just ask her agent to have a look through them and pass on any that he thought she was suitable for. With little else to do; she read them all herself.

There were so any rubbish ones!! Most would never see the light of day!

One caught her eye though. It had been written by a local author; it was a ghost story called The Miner's Lad. It was set in present day and the part she had been sent was the main female role; it was intriguing. Emma read the script then read the book and fired off an email to say she would like to audition for the part!

For Emma it felt like there would be life after Covid.

Luke picked up a slight injury and came home. He took her by surprise when he asked her to marry him.

Of course she said yes; news broke and suddenly they were inundated with offers off magazines asking if they could cover the wedding. Emma and Luke had never thought about their wedding turning into a circus; but Luke's career could be cut short at any minute and Emma; even though the door in London would always be open; still hadn't secured work for the following year. The money the magazines offered was ridiculous.

As soon as they could; Emma and Luke married at a registry office; they got the wedding they wanted with just a handful of family and friends; bizarrely all wearing masks and sitting 2 metres apart from each other. But the circus didn't come to town.

Emma Keeps who was then Emma Keep, then became her most favourite of all; Emma Chambers.

They booked a local venue; huge and picturesque for the following summer and invited a magazine for the exclusive. They knew that they were already married, but a blessing and a fabulous guest list filled with actors, actresses and footballers were all they were after. The small matter that by then they would have been married for over a year didn't bother them.

By the time that Emma Chambers said 'I do' to Luke Chambers for a second time; filming of The Miner's

Lad had finished. Emma was so proud of how the finished series looked.

Filming had taken almost 6 months longer than scheduled; mainly due to cast and crew having various outbreaks of covid. But they had persevered and what they had made was beautiful and haunting and a little bit spine chilling.

People who had seen it were talking about Emma Keep getting a Bafta for her portrayal of Grace. Time would tell.

When the series aired on prime time Sunday night; the critics agreed. Emma Keep; soap star had made the transition into serious drama. Bafta talk was back.

Emma had come a long way.

The offer of roles kept on coming. But Emma was particular; she was so happy living in Newcastle; keeping everything true to her roots; she turned them down; waited for something that more suited her style came her way.

They didn't need the money. First the series and then the Wedding had bolstered Emma and Luke's bank balance. Luke was back playing first team football; there was even talk of him going to the World Cup if he could stay injury free.

And away from everything they lived a simple life.

£10 note HE75 229564 had been money well spent.

It had given Emma hope when she thought her career was going to fail to launch.

Madame Zita had been one of the first people she saw when she came back to Newcastle; when she first rented a house when she was Cushie Butterfield.

It wasn't so much she wanted to know what happened next; it was more of a thank you. But she couldn't resist a little reading. Emma knew Luke was going to propose months before he did.

Madame Zita was a guest at their wedding; even made it into the magazine and someone who Emma now considered a friend.

Only last week Emma had sat on the stool at her kitchen table shuffling Madame Zita's cards. It was a social call, Madame Zita had called to wish Emma good look at the up and coming Bafta Event.

Predictably, it ended up in a little reading and as always Madame Zita told Emma to ask a question.

There was only one question of Emma Chamber's mind …

And there it was the Ace of Cups! The card that signifies a birth …

'Tarot Doesn't Predict the Future. Tarot Facilitates it.'
Phillipe St Genoux

19

Money for Old Rope

Jean Carson had received £10 note HE75 229564 from Emma Keeps.

Not that Emma knew Jean as Jean; for Emma and hundreds of others over the years; Jean Carson was Madame Zita. The fortune teller who foretold Emma that she would be a star; and the prediction had been proved right.

When Note Taken was being written and I was making my way back to all of the first characters of the first book; Jean Carson had refused to take part.

She was in a bad place; it was not long after Kitty, her daughter had tried to kill herself. Jean's inability to see what had been happening before her eyes as Kitty's mammy had left her riddled with guilt. More so when as Madame Zita she could foretell all sorts of things for other people; usually stupid stuff that was irrelevant really. But there had been nothing to warn her that her daughter was crippled with Postpartum Psychosis resulting in Kitty taking some broken glass and slashing at her wrists.

All Jean could think was that Kitty must have been

desperate; she herself had been so engrossed in her new granddaughter that she had let Kitty's plight slide straight passed her.

Jean had gained a granddaughter but almost lost her daughter.

It was something that Jean didn't want to talk about, even knowing that Kitty was on the road to recovery; when Jean had requested to be left out. Her request was granted.

But now she is back. In the intervening 4 years; the wounds have healed and she is happy to talk about then until now.

When Kitty had first got married and left home; Jean and Eddie decided that their house; which they had lived in for more years than they could remember was too big. It had been a family home; a home for a family of 6 not 2; and as much as they loved every square inch of it; Jean and Eddie rattled about in it.

It would fetch a fair penny; they had bought it cheap; very cheap and even if they took all of the renovations into account; they would make a killing.

But they had dithered. It was as much Jean & Eddie as their kids were. It had kept them safe and protected them. It was going to be a wrench leaving the place. They had even gone so far as to ask the kids if any of them wanted to buy it; somehow knowing that strangers wouldn't be living in it would make it less painful.

But of course they didn't; too old fashioned; too big; too small. None of them felt the same connection to the house that their mammy and daddy did.

Despite their hesitancy about selling their home; they had no idea where they wanted to live. The fact that they ran successful businesses; to all and sundry they would still be classed as gypos; not everyone liked that sort moving into their street.

They had been lucky; their house was in a street; but there was so much space between the houses that people took little notice of who lived where; it wasn't as if they tethered horses up in their front garden; but still. They were too old to be drawing attention to themselves.

So they ended up doing nothing; which in hindsight had been the right thing to do.

When Kitty took ill; Jimmy and the baby moved in. Jimmy couldn't look after baby Rosella alone; especially working full time. Jimmy and Rosella came to stay and when Kitty was well enough to come home, she stayed too.

They stayed and they never moved out.

Kitty and Jimmy made Jean and Eddie's home their home too.

The big old fashioned house was full again and all thoughts of selling it and moving on were shelved.

It worked though.

Kitty, Jean and Eddie worked in the arcades; shifts to suit Rosella.

When she was bigger; Rosella would go to the arcades too; just like Kitty's brothers had done with their children. Just like Jean had done with Kitty when she was little; it hadn't done Kitty any harm, it certainly wouldn't do Rosella any.

But Jean watched Kitty like a hawk. Not her parenting skills; she was an amazing little mammy. Jean had been so close to losing her; if it hadn't been for Jimmy she may have lost her. Jean had a lot to be grateful to Jimmy for. But despite Kitty still having to take an anti-depressant every day; she was more or less her old self. Jean could maybe think about taking a breath herself; she had been saving her breath for so long.

All the while Jean's alter-ego; Madame Zita continued to ply her trade. 4 or 5 nights a week Jean would tie back her hair and head off to someone's house for a party. Her reputation ensured that the bookings kept on coming and the coffers kept on growing.

Jean loved it. She liked to think she could help people; give them hope. Because the majority of her readings were simply that. Tapping into what someone wanted and then facilitating the right outcome. She didn't like to think that she was a con-woman; she certainly wasn't. But more often than not; her spiritual side didn't get anything off the person sitting at the opposite side of the table from her.

The cards would sometimes give her a glimmer of something; but they too would only perform for the right person.

A long time ago; when Fortune Telling had only been something that she saw in the travelling people at the shows where Jean and Eddie sold burgers at; she would often wonder what it was that they did.

Curiosity killed the cat and Jean found herself sitting in front of Gypsy Morag Lee who, Jean had noticed; always had a long queue outside. It had been a fruitless exercise as far as getting a reading was concerned; Gypsy Morag Lee deemed that Jean had more ability that she herself hid. But Jean learned so much.

Gypsy Morag Lee wasn't a trickster; far from it. She had the gift. But the gift wasn't always very giving, so it became a game of observation. She would listen to what people were saying in the queue; their hopes and aspirations. You could gleam so much she went on; people talked. 'Get the first one of the day right; you get the lot!'

There were so many ways to know about people beyond that though; dark circles usually indicated either a baby or a broken heart. Age was usually an indicator too; older tended to have lost someone. Spending time Gypsy Morag Lee was like having a masterclass.

Years later; Jean would recall all of her tips and advice; hone in her tarot card handling and Madame Zita had been born.

And just like Gypsy Morag Lee had predicted; some people did alert the spirits or activate the cards and that made Madame Zita's job a whole heap easier. Often it was just a game of skill.

It was lucrative though. Jean always like to think that Madame Zita was providing a service; hope in a world that sometimes seemed hopeless.

Over the years Jean had her regulars; they would book to see her every few months and relationships were forged. Sometimes she felt like she was more of a counsellor that a psychic; but if they crossed her palm; Jean could be anything they needed her to be.

Life as an extended family settled. Rosella thrived. Kitty thrived. Life was looking good again.

And then the arcades had to close over-night.

Madame Zita had to moth ball her crystal ball.

The virus from China had arrived in Britain and because no one knew what it was all about; everyone was put into Lockdown until they could find some answers. It made sense; people were dying. The hospitals were ram packed with people not able to breathe.

It was all very scary.

They were lucky; they had money. But as the weeks ticked away the concern began to grow for Jean and Eddie. Everyone in the family worked in the arcades in some shape or form; the three boys; their wives when they weren't having babies; Kitty. The only one that wasn't reliant on the family business was Jimmy.

There was little to be done but sit it out. The sun had shone and the family spent their days in the garden; Rosella growing like a little flower by the day in the sunshine of the garden. The nights were spent playing games or watching the latest box set.

The boys would visit; but stand at the bottom of the drive. Usually they would be there to pick some money up; a lot of their business was cash; the money that made it into the bank was to pay their overheads; so it seemed that there was always one of the boys there waiting with their hand out for some money. The stash was depleting rapidly.

Jean could see that Eddie was worried. Would it get so bad that they would not be able to afford to re-open the arcades??

The Government stepped in though. There was money to be had and Jean and Eddie applied for everything and anything they could.

Their lively hood was reprieved but with little chance of the arcades anytime soon with all the restrictions in place even after they had been relaxed; they still had to be careful.

But then Madame Zita came to the rescue again.

Kitty had seen on social media that people were offering telephone readings. Jean had no idea how that would even work. The whole 'fortune telling' malarkey was 30% spirit 70% observation. How could she do that over the telephone!!

Jimmy to the rescue. 'If you advertise on Facebook, then they will have a Facebook profile!'

It worked out perfectly.

Kitty made Madame Zita an account and bang; they were inundated with messages off people wanting to book appointments.

Between them; Kitty and Jean set up a booking

system; people paid directly into the bank account; which was a little alarming for Jean; Madame Zita had never really been an official business. But the money was there and she would speak to their accountant about being able to run Madame Zita as being part of the arcades entertainment.

People would book, pay their money and Kitty or Jimmy would research them. It was amazing how much information about people could be gleamed off their profile. Where they worked; so they would know if they were currently working or furloughed. Who they were in a relationship with. Who their children were. It was an encyclopaedia of personal knowledge and before each call; the narrative would be read and Jean had an idea who she was doing the reading for.

The strangest thing though was sometimes the spirits would come. They would whisper in her ear and tell her what the person on the other end of the phone needed to know!

Other times the cards would have the answers.

It was a ritual with each call.

'Lovely I am going to shuffle the cards; tell me when you feel I should stop.'

'Lovely, I have split the cards into three piles; please think hard and choose a number'.

'Lovely, I have spread the cards. I am going to hover my hands over the cards. Tell me when to stop.'

The customers did this. Sometimes they would want

three cards, sometimes more. Madame Zita didn't mind, they had paid for a 30 minute call.

Sometimes calls would last a little longer. Always the counsellor; Madame Zita would never end a call if someone was upset. The more Madame Zita made telephone readings, the more she realised that basically people were just lonely.

Many hadn't seen their families for months and months. Lockdown and the virus had a lot to answer for.

Madame Zita helped where she could. It was the old hope thing. Yes you will see your family again. Yes, your family are all doing fine. Yes you will meet someone once the. restrictions are lifted 'I can see him now, standing with his arm around your shoulders!' it went on and on.

All this hope for £30 for 30 minutes. It was cheaper than therapy.

The telephone readings is something that is part of Madame Zita's service these days.

All ran by the more than capable Kitty who books the calls in for her mammy for when she isn't out doing parties.

Because once restrictions lifted; everyone wanted their fortunes told! It had all been so hopeless for so long!

The arcades were in the last tier of businesses to be reopened. Even when they did they were bloody hard work; social distancing; policing masks; the constant wiping down of the machines; but it was some kind of normality and they were all grateful.

LAST NOTE

Jean Carson was grateful for so much.

That all her family had made it through a pandemic unscathed; not one of them had caught the dreaded lurgy.

Grateful that their business had survived.

Grateful for her new grandson Bruno who had arrived just one week earlier to Kitty and Jimmy. A little brother for Rosella!

Madame Zita had kept the till ringing; but she had given them more than that; she had given them some sort of normality in a time when there was so much uncertainty and fear. She had given her customers so much hope but she had got back so much more than money.

Madame Zita had given them purpose!

When Emma Keeps had handed £10 note HE75 229564 over to Madame Zita and in return Madame Zita had given Emma Keeps hope; she had no idea that what Madame Zita had told her had been fact or fiction. But it gave her the hope to believe in herself.

It had been one of Madame Zita's one true predictions and the proof had been in the pudding when Emma Keeps won the illusive part. For Emma Keeps the rest was history. Jean watched her career with relish; local girl done good.

And over the years Emma and Jean had developed a relationship.

For Emma it was paying her friend back when she had invited Madame Zita to her celebrity wedding.

Madame Zita photograph had made it into the glossy

magazine and her name was out there. 'Fortune Teller of the Stars' had been the tag line!

The telephone had been ringing off the hook.

It seemed it didn't make any difference how famous or rich you were; everyone needed hope.

Just take today!!!

There was a message on the fridge with a contact number off someone called Boris ….. !!!!

'Hope is Being Able to See Light Despite All of the Darkness.'

Desmond Tutu

20

More Money Than Sense!

When Kitty Carson had fell in love with Jimmy Watson there had been only one way that she knew of to tell it to the world. A tattoo!!

£10 note HE75 229564 had been part of the advance in wages Kitty had got off her mammy; Jean Carson aka Madame Zita when she needed the cash to pay for the tattoo.

Her mammy and daddy knew nothing about Kitty getting a tattoo and they knew nothing of Kitty being in love with Jimmy either.

Kitty had really not known how to tell them. It wasn't that they wouldn't approve; Kitty was their youngest but not just the youngest; she was there only daughter. Always the diva; Kitty had thought she could coast through life when she left school; that she would be handed money for clothes and stuff just like she always had.

But her mammy and daddy were having none of it and when she failed to materialise a job using her own devices; they made her work in one of the arcades they ran.

Kitty had kicked and screamed; that had been the last place she wanted to work; but it was their way or the highway. No arcade then no money. Party animal Kitty had no option; it wasn't just the nights out; it would be clothes and shoes and the million and one other things that she got and up until that point had really taken for granted.

For Kitty it had been shocking to be told she had to go and work in one of the dumps they called the arcade. She had gone to her brothers; pleaded her point; but they were having none of it either. They worked in the places she called dumps; short change off them and with little hope of securing a job of her own; she went.

On hindsight it was the best move she could ever had made. Working at the arcade brought her Jimmy.

It had been love at first sight. One look and that was it; she was gone. Jimmy had been who she had been waiting for. All the bad kissing with school boys; drunkenly losing her virginity in Ibiza; all the things that she should have been loving and felt nothing for had been leading to the point when Jimmy Watson walked into the arcade and Kitty fell in love.

And with that lay the problem. The not telling anyone about Jimmy thing.

But the tattoo; the beautiful little tattoo that she had in between her shoulder blades was the testament to a love like she had never known before. A love that was reciprocated from Jimmy.

With the tattoo in place; Kitty had walked into the

back room of the arcade where she knew her mammy and daddy would be together.

It was out of her mouth before they had even had chance to say hello. 'Mammy, Daddy this is Jimmy and I love her. Her real name is Jemima Louise Watson but you can call her Jimmy!' With that, Kitty had turned on her heels and flounced out of their office pulling a shocked looking Jimmy behind her.

Jimmy Watson was a girl.

Kitty had known that she was a girl that first time she saw her; but most people went on first impressions though and Jimmy looked like a boy. She had short hair; wore boys clothes and had all of the swagger of any young lad her age.

Not long after they started going out Kitty had asked Jimmy if she thought that she was in the wrong body. Expecting confirmation off Jimmy that she would like nothing better than to have a sex change, Kitty was shocked when Jimmy said no. She was happy with what God had given her. She just liked to dress masculine. She didn't want a penis and even confessed to Kitty that when they were in bed; she liked Kitty to touch her boobs.

Kitty had never been happier.

It had taken a little time for Jean Carson to get used to the idea of Kitty being with a girl; Eddie Carson even longer. But seeing how happy Kitty was; how good Jimmy was with her sealed the deal and in no time; her mammy and daddy were used to their daughter's choice of boyfriend.

Kitty wanted it all though; she wanted to be with Jimmy forever and when she realised that they could legally marry; she wanted that too,

Usually what Kitty wanted she got.

So, Kitty got her lavish wedding and became Mrs Watson.

Her mammy and daddy gave them the flat above the town centre arcade and life could not have been better.

Until Jimmy's sister announced that she was pregnant.

It was the one thing that Kitty could never have. But it hit her like a tonne of bricks; she had never really thought about being a mammy herself; she had just been so wrapped up in Jimmy. And the truth of it was that she had so many nieces and nephews that if anything that would put her off kids; those lot would. They were feral!!!

But she was eaten up with jealousy as Lucy's pregnancy progressed.

It made her something that she had never been before. Sad. Her mammy and daddy had looked after her so well there had never been a day when her life had been more sad than happy. Maybe the odd occasion when some kids she went to school with called her a pykie or a gypo. But Kitty always had the last laugh; she had so much more than they could ever have had; the ever changing wardrobe; the warm welcome from her mammy and daddy for any friends who visited. So this whole not having a baby thing was killing her.

It was Lucy who broke Kitty and got her to talk. It was Lucy who told her that it wasn't impossible for to have a baby; they just had to think outside the box.

When she had plucked up enough courage she spoke to Jimmy about having a baby. It seemed she had already opened that box; she wanted a baby too. And she had a sperm donor already lined up.

Kitty could not believe she had been stupid enough not to speak to Jimmy about it. She had everything already sorted. Jimmy's cousin Tommy had offered when Jimmy had first got together with Kitty; Jimmy just had to say the word.

Tommy was perfect. Jimmy and Tommy were images of each other. Jimmy was tall for a girl, Tommy short for a boy; they had the same haircut and the same swagger.

They all researched what needed to be done and after a botched up first attempt; the second worked and Kitty and Jimmy Watson were going to be parents.

A baby girl no less.

Her mammy and daddy were a little shocked; but before they knew it the flat began to fill up with all things pink from Jean and Eddie and the arrival of their granddaughter could not have come quick enough.

Rosella arrived in the presence of her mammy Jimmy and her grandma Jean.

A little on the small side; Kitty was nervous about handling her tiny daughter. The midwife tried to help

Kitty feed her; Rosella wouldn't have any of it. They decided on a bottle so Jimmy and her mammy did that; old wives tale or not, Kitty was grateful that it wasn't the done thing to bottle feed a baby anywhere near its mammy with her milk.

By the time they were discharged from the hospital; Kitty had barely touched her daughter, she was terrified of her. Scared in case she hurt her tiny body; dropped her; the things that could happen scared Kitty stiff.

Home everyone oooh'ed and aaarh'ed and no one realised that she didn't touch Rosella. The nearest she got was to stare at her in her crib or pram.

The fear was starting to cripple her.

Kitty did everything she could not to be left alone with her.

Jimmy just thought that Kitty was tired after the ordeal of carrying the baby and giving birth; she was happy to take on the role of mammy while Kitty pulled herself together.

If anyone came; Kitty put on a face; but once they left, she would lie on the settee or take to her bed. She would cry silent tears when she heard Jimmy with Rosella in the next room, or in the bathroom. Jimmy was a natural.

Kitty fell deeper and deeper into her black hole of despondency.

No one seemed to notice. Baby blues they would have thought.

By the time Jimmy was due to go back to work; Kitty was mortally terrified. There was no way that she could look after Rosella on her own. Rosella would be dead in a week.

The black cloud got darker and thicker and heavier.

The night before Jimmy was due to go back to work; Kitty went into the bathroom; smashed a glass and slit both her wrists. Then there was true blackness.

Postpartum Psychosis they said when she eventually woke and talked. She was so ashamed of herself. She could barely look at her family. Especially Jimmy. But the psychiatrist explained all about why she had been feeling like she had. It was not Kitty's fault; she was ill.

Postpartum Psychosis is a mental illness that can affect you in the first weeks after giving birth. Symptoms appear suddenly, sense of reality can be lost and hallucinations, delusions, mood swings and behaviour changes.

A specialist unit was found and Kitty was transferred and her recovery began.

It was going to be a long road; Kitty was given a cocktail of tablets including anti-depressants and sleeping tablets.

Kitty would cry; her emotions still hard to keep in check, especially as there were other new mothers on the unit and some of them were allowed to have their babies with them.

Kitty cried for Rosella. She missed her so much.

Jimmy would bring little videos of Rosella in when

she visited and every time Kitty saw one she could see Rosella changing. Jean had insisted that Jimmy and Rosella move in with her and Eddie, it made sense, Jimmy still had to go to work. It was nice to think that the family were rallying around and Rosella was being well cared for.

Kitty slowly improved. Her mammy visited and then Rosella. This time Kitty wasn't afraid; she cuddled her tiny baby in. She had missed her baby so much.

Home visits followed and then Rosella came to stay with her mammy at the unit. It was the first time Kitty had Rosella on her own since she was born. She was so scared that Rosella wouldn't remember her and fret to go home. But she had bathed her and fed her and soothed her to sleep. Kitty forgot all about the nurses watching her; she just revelled in the chance to love her daughter.

And then she was well enough to go home. She was still taking her anti-depressants and there would be a monthly review to judge her state of mind; but Kitty knew herself that she was feeling better. It made Kitty shudder when she thought about the night that had led to her admittance. If she hadn't fainted and clattered her head off the door, Jimmy may not have found her until it was too late.

Kitty and Jimmy stayed with her mammy and daddy. It made sense. She still had the odd day when she would sleep longer in the morning or would need an afternoon nap; it was just the tablets but still, it was better having someone else there to take care of Rosella when Kitty wasn't up for it.

The good thing to come out of her being away at the unit was that Jimmy and her mammy and daddy got chance to bond. By the time Kitty got home, Jimmy was very much part of the family, not that she hadn't been before, they had welcomed her as they did everyone who visited their home. Now though there was a real relationship there; genuine and loving, forged over their love for Kitty and Rosella.

The scars on Kitty's arms healed; some of them had been quite deep; but they were nothing in comparison with the scar this whole ordeal had left on Kitty's heart. If she lived a hundred years she could never make it up to Jimmy and her mammy and daddy. They cared for her as if she was made of porcelain. Each seemed to be riddled with guilt that they carried needlessly. They thought they had missed Kitty's distress. The truth of it was, Kitty was good at hiding it.

There was no blame anywhere. It was just one of those things.

Kitty and Rosella both continued to thrive daily.

By the time Rosella was celebrating her 1st birthday; Kitty was almost back to her pre-drama days.

Rosella was a little diamond. She lit up the house with her continuous chatter and laughter; despite their enforced separation at the beginning of Rosella's little life; there was no broken bond; even when Kitty returned to work at the arcade a few hours a week; Rosella went with her.

Kitty and Jimmy found that they were happy living

with Kitty's mammy and daddy's. There was plenty of room; Rosella had a room of her own; and mammy and daddy were always happy to look after Rosella if Kitty and Jimmy had the odd night out.

Life was good.

And then Lockdown came and everyone was in the house all of the time together.

In the beginning it was fun. The days were warm and the nights found them playing games or just chilling watching the latest must watch on the television.

Mammy cooked delicious food; it was nice that she had time to make it and it was even nicer that they all sat around the table and ate it leisurely without anywhere else to be. But Kitty could see that mammy and daddy were worried. They had money but the whole family were being supported by it and it wouldn't last forever.

Daddy talked about losing the arcades.

The news was all bleak; there was funding on the way; but with no sign of businesses that weren't essential had no clear indication of when they would be re-opening again. An amusement arcade certainly wasn't an essential business.

It had been Jimmy that suggested that maybe Madame Zita could do telephone readings; lots of businesses were adapting with the restrictions; why should fortune telling be any different. Some fortune tellers had been doing it that way for years.

Mammy wasn't convinced. How would she see the

signs of what her clients wanted if she couldn't see them.

Facebook profiles of course. They were a mine of information.

Kitty launched a Facebook page and the customers came.

Jimmy and Kitty controlled the bookings and the narrative; they both found it interesting finding out about the clients. They would patiently type up each customer's information and Madame Zita would use it to glean what the person on the other end of the phone wanted; no needed to hear.

Her Mammy said they needed hope; Kitty thought they needed amusement.

How the bookings came in.

Kitty encouraged reviews on the Facebook Page and within weeks customers were coming from far and wide; way beyond anywhere Madame Zita had plied her trade pre-covid.

Even when Jimmy returned to work; Kitty took on the role of Madame Zita's administrator; she loved it.

It was so lucrative that Kitty began to receive a weekly wage off Madame Zita. It was a good feeling. Something beyond the arcades.

Eventually daddy had got the okay for the arcades to re-open; they had made it. It was all hands on deck to run them so Kitty found herself very busy; between the arcade and Madame Zita; it was almost a full time job.

Even when Madame Zita went back out to do

parties; the telephone service continued. It was too lucrative not to. £30 for 30 mins work. Mammy was more than happy to do a couple of mornings an afternoon and an odd evening.

Life once again took on a steady beat.

The scars on her arms would never fade completely, but they were who she was. The doctors had told her that in their opinion she should never have another baby; there was no guarantee that the same thing wouldn't happen again; it was a needless risk to take. Rosella was everything they would ever need.

Or so Kitty had thought.

Whether it was because of the covid pandemic; or whether it was because once restrictions lifted and Rosella's cousins could come over and play with her, Jimmy thought it may be a good idea if they could have another baby.

Kitty was gob-smacked. She had thought that Jimmy was happy with how things were. Jimmy was she stressed; but each of them had brothers and sisters; they didn't even really know anyone that didn't. She just didn't want Rosella to miss out.

There was no way that Kitty could have a baby.

But Jimmy could she said.

It had been something that Kitty thought she would ever have heard Jimmy say. But she was right; she had all the same bits and bobs as Kitty did; it would make perfect sense. This time they wouldn't be able to ask

Tommy; Jimmy's cousin; that wouldn't have been right, but there would be someone and there was. This time it was her mammy's cousin's son; not as close to Kitty as Tommy was to Jimmy, but nevertheless he had offered and they weren't going to look a gift horse in the mouth.

Bingo; first time success for Jimmy and baby number two was on the way.

Poor Jimmy. Every morning she was sick as a dog; every night she had heartburn. Whereas Kitty had sailed through her pregnancy; Jimmy certainly didn't bloom. For the first three months she really struggled.

As Jimmy's bump grew, so did the stares; she looked like a pregnant boy. Even at appointments the midwives would assume it was Kitty they were seeing, the look on their faces when Jimmy answered the name call was priceless; it became sport for Kitty and Jimmy.

This time they were having a boy! One of each; they were so lucky.

Kitty fretted about what would happen after the baby was born; what if the same thing happened to Jimmy and Kitty didn't see it. What if Jimmy did something silly and Kitty lost her.

But she needn't have worried. Bruno Watson arrived at a healthy 8lbs.

Kitty had never loved Jimmy as much as she did as she sat at Jimmy's bedside nursing their new son. It was a strange sight. Kitty could actually see what Jimmy would have looked like if she didn't dress and act like a boy all of the time.

In them moments; just after Bruno was born, Jimmy looked like the Jemimah that she had been named.

Wearing a hospital gown; her usual short cropped hair hadn't been cut for a few weeks; Jimmy was too tired to go to the barbers and she'd had enough of Kitty's cuts in lockdown to let her wife anywhere near her with the clippers again. The hair was longer and curling and the look on her face was feminine; after all she had just done the most womanly thing she could ever have done in giving life.

It was surreal and time that Kitty would hold in her heart forever.

There was none of the blues that had befallen on Kitty.

They had simply gone home and began their life as a family of four.

Rosella loved the baby boy doll that was her baby brother. Kitty hadn't been sure about calling him Bruno; it had been Jimmy's choice. Named after some footballer who had been signed for Newcastle; Jimmy said he was going to be a local hero and for her it was a no brainer. He suited it. He was big and strong and he was going to be their hero; seemed fitting.

Kitty's mammy and daddy were ecstatic.

And somewhere in the mix; Kitty's mammy had become somewhat of a celebrity all thanks to Emma Keeps.

Emma Keeps who years earlier had a reading off

Madame Zita. Kitty could clearly remember the night her mammy had come home and said that she had met a young girl who was set for stardom. The spirits had told her. At the time her mammy had no idea who she was; but the minute Valentine Mitchell had turned up in Kitty's favourite soap opera; Kitty had shouted of her mammy to come see and it was her.

They had both watched Emma Keeps career explode. The footballer boyfriend. The drama she was in about some wife from Newcastle and more recently some really spooky series which put the willies up Kitty.

But Emma had sought out her mammy to thank her and they became friends. Kitty had met her a few times; Emma was very normal for such a household name; she was Kitty's claim to fame.

Never more so than when Madame Zita got invited to Emma and Luke's wedding at some swanky estate in Northumberland.

Kitty was so proud of her mammy.

When a picture of her mammy was published in the magazine that had the exclusive of the wedding; the phone didn't stop ringing; people wanting to book readings; newspapers wanting to interview her mammy; even the local television news team wanting to come and interview Madame Zita; Fortune Teller to the Stars.

Exciting times.

It had been quite a journey for the Carson/Watson family since £10 note HE75 229564 had crossed their palms. The money itself had made little difference to

Kitty; at the time she had earned it. But what it was used for symbolised Kitty's life; the little tattoo that was nestled between her shoulder blades. The expression of her love for Jimmy; the love of her life who may not have been what her mammy and daddy had expected for their only daughter but whole heartly accepted Jimmy and everything she had gave and continued to give to Kitty. Priceless!!

'Life Throws Challenges and Every Challenge Comes With Rainbows and Light to Conquer it.'

Amit Ray

21

Love of Money is the Root of All Evil

Lola Harrison knew Kitty and Jimmy well.

It had been Lola who had tattooed the space between Kitty's shoulder blades when she wanted the world to know that she was in love with Jimmy.

It was a beautiful piece.

Jimmy had been a regular at Tats for Tarts since Lola had opened it. She had been there for so many of her tattoos; many designed by herself. With each new design Jimmy brought in for Lola to tattoo; she was blown away. The girl had talent.

For Lola Harrison it had been the right move setting up on her own with a business exclusively for women. It was a safe environment for women to have even the most delicate areas tattooed. When Lola had approached the banks with her business plan they had told her it wouldn't work; that she was halving her potential client base.

But how wrong they had been.

Women of all shapes and sizes came. Many said they had always wanted a tattoo but were put off going into tattooists; the shops had a certain sort of reputation.

Tats for Tarts offered them something different. Privacy; a guaranteed women tattooist and a safe environment to be in.

The business thrived.

Lola loved it. It was hard work; especially with a family at home to care for too. But her husband Anthony helped out loads with the boys and did his fair share of housework.

Everyone was always surprised that Lola was married. More so married to a man and then even more so when they met Anthony. Lola and Anthony were chalk and cheese. Lola with her tattoos and piercings and wildly coloured hair and scruffy clothes could not be any further removed from Anthony who looked every inch the financial advisor he was. Even when he wasn't wearing a suit; he was a controlled dresser; matching sweatshirt and joggers; nice jeans with a nice top. For being married to one of Newcastle's most recognised tattooists; he didn't have a single one; not even a pierced ear.

But they worked. They first hooked up at a party in Uni and the rest was history. Anthony moved 300 miles to be with Lola. He was the Ying to her Yang.

Tommy and Billy had followed and even though they were so close in age, size and looks; by the time they hit their teens; they too were Ying to the other ones Yang!

When Lola Harrison and Tats for Tarts was featured in a national tattoo magazine; the shop boomed.

The feature had depicted a very honest Lola

LAST NOTE

Harrison with her family along with Kitty, Jimmy and Rosella. It may have been a feature on Lola but it had been Kitty Watson and her tattoo who had made the front cover!! A stunning girl with a stunning tattoo.

Business boomed and just as Lola thought that it was maybe time for her to take on another tattooist; the pandemic arrived and the Lola found herself locking up her little shop with no idea when it would be re-opening.

Home became their Haven.

With no idea what was going on; like the rest of the Nation; they watched the daily Government news briefings religiously.

The death rates rose, and the Lockdown lengthened. And all the while no one had any idea what was going on.

Tommy and Billy were loving their lives. No school; days spent on their Xboxes eating their mam and dad out of house and home. But even the Xboxes lost their appeal and they would spend the days in the garden; kicking a football or basically being busy doing nothing.

As the weeks ticked on Lola could see Anthony becoming more and more worried. He was a spreadsheet sort of bloke and all the uncertainty didn't suit him.

Lola was more a fly by the seat of your pants type of girl; of course she worried about stuff; Tommy and Billy were a constant worry; not so much in lockdown when she had a fair idea what they were getting up to. But even then, how was the enforced imprisonment affecting them and their mental health. How was it not if affecting their schoolwork and their impeding exams; Tommy was due to sit his GCSE's in the summer; Billy the year after. What would happen now with there being no school?

When the news came that not only was there going to be assistance for shopkeepers; but Anthony would be able to work; abate from home and the boys were going to have some shape of schooling starting in the next few week; the relief for Anthony and Lola was tangible.

Anthony made an office for himself in their dining room; which had been having a fair bit of use over the past weeks; it had been nice them all sitting around the dining table eating together; in normal times they tended to eat in the kitchen or in front of the telly and then they ate at different times depending on who was doing what. The dining table was mainly used at Christmas and that was that.

But it was gone again; Anthony had envisaged that he was going to be very busy; the Government were introducing some sort of interruption loan and Anthony's company had been earmarked as one of the banks to facilitate them.

The boys luckily each had laptops so they would be able to work in their rooms.

The house took on a different tempo; one that Lola had no part of. Anthony worked, Tommy and Billy did school work.

Lola was left to her own devices and she didn't like it.

Usually, her own life was flat out. Home to shop;

shop to home via the supermarket. Housework and cooking really wasn't doing it for her. Lola was bored and had no idea how to amuse herself.

She was unsure if she could be in her shop but went anyway.

It looked so neglected; Lola set about a spring clean; did all the jobs that she never seemed to have time to do in her daily life; bit of paint here fixed a squeaky door there.

It was so sad. The whole street looked forlorn. The only sign of life was the bins outside the takeaway shops which were full to bursting.

All Lola could do was watch for restriction updates and wait. There was money in the bank to pay the bills; thanks to money off the Government; the shop was ship shape and Bristol fashion and as soon as they said go; she was ready.

At home she cooked for her boys; Anthony hardly got chance to catch breath while he was logged on to his laptop; but she made sure they all had drinks and snacks and there was a hearty meal ready for them at the end of the day.

It was the strangest of times.

Social media was the only avenue she had for keeping her brand out there. Lola posted designs; tips and advice about choosing the right design; care for tattoos.

And still they waited. They clapped on their doorsteps every Thursday night and when the lifting of restrictions began; Lola waited patiently to see when she could once again open the door of Tats for Tarts.

When the date for re-opening was announced; Lola was inundated with messages and telephone calls off clients wanting to book in. it was going to be zero to flat out from the get go.

Lola couldn't be happier.

Getting another tattooist would have been idea; but she would ride it out herself; if the mad rush was literally just that and if the bubble burst and trade slowed down; she didn't want to have the pressure of an additional wage she couldn't afford. Things were still far from normal; she could wait.

Jimmy Watson was a little bit of a life saver. She would call at the shop often; help out by keeping the shop clean and tidy while Lola worked and brought with her the most amazing designs. Jimmy really was a very talented artist.

Jimmy would make an amazing tattooist; something Lola said to her on many occasions; food for thought she told Jimmy. Lola really could see herself sharing her workspace with Jimmy; and she was a walking advertisement for the shop; Lola had done almost all of Jimmy's body art work.

When Emma Keep called to book in a private consultation, Lola was blown away. THE Emma Keep wanted to come to Tats for Tarts; she had any tattooist in the country to choose from; but she had said on the phone that she had seen the article in the magazine;

again Lola was blown away.

Emma came at the end of the day; the shop was empty apart from Lola and Jimmy and Emma brought along her boyfriend; who too was a household name that Lola had never heard of but Jimmy was total in awe of and stood open mouthed when the young couple came into the shop.

Turned out that Emma and Luke were getting married; all very hush hush; they were having a lavish celebrity wedding the following year; so the official one they were having at a registry office was being kept under the radar. But they wanted to mark the occasion and thought that having matching tattoos would be a perfect way to mark their official wedding day.

Jimmy was all over it; she did 3 beautiful designs; each as perfect as the next and Emma and Luke must have found it hard to choose because it took them days to decide and book in for their appointments.

The finished tattoos were some of Lola's finest work. Not that she ever did a bad job; it was more that they had turned out identical. Perfect. It was such a shame that the tattoos wouldn't see the light of day. To the world they weren't even married.

When Jimmy said that she would like to become a tattooist Lola was over the moon. She would be an asset to the business; with her flair for design; Jimmy would be bringing something extra to Tat for Tarts that other tattoo shops didn't have.

But just as they were about to embark on the

training; Jimmy blew Lola way.

Jimmy was having a baby.

The words were something that Lola had never envisaged Jimmy speaking. But after the drama of Kitty's life after the arrival of Rosella there was no way that Kitty could risk making herself ill again. It made sense; Jimmy was a girl too. And Lola would happily wait for Jimmy to have the baby before embarking on her training. Jimmy would be the best; she would be worth the wait.

What a strange sight it was though. Jimmy dressed like a boy and her ever growing bump. Sometimes Jimmy just looked like a fat lad; others it was unmistakable that she was having a baby. Lola could see people doing double takes. Funny!

And all the while she waited for Jimmy to have her baby; the shop continued to thrive. The bubble that had exploded when restrictions had been lifted hadn't popped.

Life at home continued much the same. Tommy and Billy went back to school in a mismatch of school and home tutoring. Anthony continued to take up their dining room table with no sign of him ever returning to his office. At least with him being at home Lola didn't need to worry so much about being home for the boys.

Emma Keep and Luke Chambers married.

Jimmy and Kitty broke their necks to bring Lola a copy of the magazine that had been given exclusive rights to the wedding.

Ten pages of the stars; their family and friends. Footballers; actors. There was a lovely photograph of Kitty's mam who Lola never knew was Madame Zita; Lola had always been a sceptic but had always heard good things about Madame Zita.

And then there was THE photograph.

Emma and Luke's matching tattoos; a symbol of their love. The blurb underneath mentioned Lola Harrison and Tats for Tarts and it mentioned the designer; Jimmy Watson.

If Lola thought that the business had exploded when restrictions lifted; it was nothing in comparison to what happened after the magazine was published with Emma and Luke's wedding in.

Suddenly Tats for Tarts was national and people were booking from all over the place. But it hadn't just been clients; the local press wanting interviews and she had a couple of phone calls off tattooists enquiring about vacancies. It would still be months before Jimmy would be able to start her training; it would make sense to have a qualified tattooist in place sooner than that.

Lola and Jimmy interviewed two girls. Both very experienced; both working in mainstream shops. Each was as good as the other. Lola liked them both. Jimmy thought they were both skilled.

The shop was big enough; Lola took on them both.

The demand was there; Lola hated turning clients away; hated even booking them in for two months later.

It had been a good decision. Louise and Cindy were the perfect fit.

Lola Harrison had been the last person to have £10 note HE75 229564 before it went back into the bank; into circulation and forever gone!

It had not made a huge different to Lola; tattoos were expensive and she often got paid in cash.

Lola who had taken a leap of faith and had managed to land herself on a cloud. Lola who had courage in her conviction when others said it wouldn't work.

Tats for Tarts; tattooist to the stars; that says it all!

*'At All Stages of Life, Own Your Choices.
Have Courage of Conviction!'*
Priyanka Chopra

22

Whip Round!

Wendy Carr had unfortunately never touched £10 note HE75 229564.

In celebration of her 50th birthday; a group of her friends had done a little whip round and the result was a little tattoo on her shoulder courtesy of Lola at Tats for Tarts.

Lola had been sure that she had handed over £10 note HE75 229564 in Wendy's change, but she had forgot that Wendy Carr had tipped her generously, the £10 note had ended up in Tats for Tarts banking and the chain was broken.

But Wendy had told her story anyway and it seems fitting that a little catch up was on the cards.

Wendy Carr had been newly divorced and embracing not just her fabulous 50s but life as a single female.

She had been married to Keith for over 25 years; with him almost 30 and thought that was her life. She had raised two lovely kids, she emphasised, she had raised them. Keith worked hard; too hard she thought at times; so it had been housewife Wendy's job to make sure the kids were fit and well.

LAST NOTE

The kids left home and with time on her hands and with no urge or need to get herself a job; Wendy had taken up golf and found that she was pretty good at it. Not a professional standard; but the members seemed to like playing against the newbie; which Wendy took as a compliment.

They said Wendy had an eye for the ball; the only trouble was she had taken her eye off marriage and Keith left.

It sounded simpler than it actually was. Keith had been having an affair with his secretary for years. There had been no tell tale signs; everything was just as it always had been; even Keith's long absences abroad sourcing materials for his company; it was something he had always done.

His lust for his wife hadn't stopped; allegedly that was one of the first signs that your husband was cheating. But even the night before he had told Wendy he was leaving; they had been on the kitchen bench; just like they had always been; they took opportunity to be intimate whenever they could. Keith obviously didn't feel like he was cheating on Katie with Wendy.

But he had gone and a bit later so had their marital home.

Wendy could honestly say that neither of these mammoth losses from her life made Wendy feel sad. She certainly didn't miss the big detached house; and she didn't really miss Keith.

The kids had fretted; they watched her like a hawk

in the early days, waiting for the breakdown that never came.

If anything Wendy Carr was happier.

She played golf whenever she wanted; even having golfing holidays with her new golf ladies and once the house was sold and she had moved into a smaller rented accommodation she could honestly say she felt something like contentment.

Keith had married Katie; Special K Wendy called them and looking at their wedding photographs on some beach somewhere hot; Wendy had felt nothing. If Keith was happy then all was good. Life was too short for envy and especially being envious of Keith's new wife; she had been there and done that and now had a life of her own.

Wendy played golf; she played a lot of golf.

When she wasn't playing golf she would socialise in the 19th hole or if anyone was organising anything; meals out, theatre, cinema; then Wendy would go too.

Keith had been generous with the profits out of the house; she had never contributed financially, but she had allowed Keith to work by being the kids' main carer; she didn't need to work. But when they were looking for staff for the 19th hole at the golf course; Wendy had applied for it and surprisingly got it.

People told her that they weren't surprised that she got the job; she was a people person and quickly became a valued member of staff.

Wendy loved it.

Being a barmaid played to her strengths. She had an ear to listen; a mouth that kept shut when it needed to be and she could flirt for England.

When Keith had first left, Wendy missed the sex. It was something she had never had to go out and find for herself; she had always just been a one man women. But singledom was different.

After all she was a lady in her 50s; but whereas she listened to some of her friends and sex was something that they avoided at all costs. Wendy couldn't get enough.

And it came to her in all shapes and forms. The golf course was a hotbed of men and Wendy sampled quite a few of them.

Sex was something that she had no hang-ups about. Her body was in better shape than it had been before she had been a mother; mainly thanks to the amount of golf she played; but getting naked didn't phase her at all.

What did phase her was the amount of men that wanted to have a relationship with her just because she'd had sex. It was the last thing Wendy wanted; her motto of 'Good times; not long times!' was her mantra.

But then she met Adam and something changed within her.

Adam was a painter and decorator and had been recommended to her by one of her friends at the golf club. She had been regaling them about her wallpaper in the living room; she said she had never noticed until she was entertaining one night and her companion had said that the room was wonky. The wallpaper hadn't been put on straight. Once she had seen it; Wendy couldn't unsee it and now it was driving her mad.

Judy had said that Adam was good; fair price and was a bit eye candy for the ladies if she knew what she meant.

Wendy wasn't bothered about him being eye candy; all she wanted was the blasted wallpaper changed.

Adam turned up a few days later to give her an estimate; Jude had been right he was a bit of a of eye candy for the ladies, but he did agree about the wallpaper; Adam said it would have driven him nuts. With price agreed it only remained for Wendy to get the paper off and get her materials.

She did; she text him to tell him that she was ready whenever he was and that began the most bizarre beginning to a friendship Wendy had ever had.

They text each other. Not just about the wonky wallpaper; but their lives, their loves. They text each other constantly.

Adam told Wendy all about Kate; about her shunning him out of her life after the death of her nan. How he was living back at his mams. He told her about Katie's dad and brothers dying in a car crash; Wendy could actually remember the story. The poor girl. Wendy offered advice; hang in there; she will come around. And Wendy found herself telling Adam all about Keith.

By the time Adam came to the house to decorate; it

was like they had known each other all of their lives.

Adam looked like he should have been Cock of the North but all Wendy could see was vulnerability. Something was stirring within her but she swallowed it down and gave herself a shake. Adam Mitchell was in his 30s what the hell would he make of a middle aged woman lusting after him; not that she thought that he hadn't been with an older woman before; he had been a bit of a lad back in the day. But still.

It was a fun week though having Adam there; it was even nice having him there when she got back from work or golf. She would always turn up with a treat for him and that would give her an excuse to make a cuppa and sit him down for 10 minutes.

When they weren't together they were texting each other. Wendy wondered what would happen when he finished the decorating.

Wendy couldn't think about it; something like panic would rise in her; she didn't know how she would feel about losing contact with him.

But he had a girlfriend who he loved; she would have been his wife if her nan hadn't died. Sooner or later they would make their way back to each other. It was an inevitable conclusion.

How Wendy wanted him though. She was sure that if Adam looked hard enough he would be able to see it.

The room was finished. This time the wallpaper was circles; Wendy loved it. She loved it more when Adam said it was like her, full of fizz. Wendy was in no doubt that Adam had seen the look of pure lust in her eyes when she had turned her head to laugh with him.

And then he was gone.

Before she knew it she was running outside to his van thanking him for decorating the living room, thanking him for saying that it reminded him of her and asking him to work his magic on her stairs and hallway.

Wendy could just not say goodbye.

It was a feeling she had never had before.

Even the men at the golf club who would normally pique her interest with their flirting held no appeal. All her thinking was rightly or wrongly of Adam.

Their messages continued. No subject was off limits. Wendy knew all about Adam having been to prison; it just made him more interesting in Wendy's eyes; she had never met anyone who had been to jail before.

Wendy told him about the men since her divorce. The ones she had slept with; the ones that tried to sleep with her even when they were well aware that Wendy was friends with their wives. There were so many layers to their friendship.

Adam came back to decorate the hallway and stairs; within the first hour they were in bed.

It was of no odds that she was a lot older than him. They fit perfectly. Wendy called it joy ride; he loved that.

While Adam decorated they had sex when they wanted. But it was more than that; Wendy now had a best friend; a lover; an everything and Adam felt the same way. The sex was mind blowing; but it ran deeper.

If Wendy was soppy enough, she might have said that they were soulmates. Adam completed her.

Even after the decorating was done they continued where they left off.

Even when Kate got back in touch they carried on.

Wendy encouraged Adam to spend time with Kate; there was no such thing as a future for Wendy with him; she was a joy ride, a one that she would either crash and burn in or one that she could slow down and get out of before anyone was hurt.

She just wasn't ready to give him up just then.

Adam courted Katie and spent time with Wendy.

And then covid arrived which was strange for everyone; no golf was bad enough, but Adam had said that Kate had asked him to move back into her mam's house with her. Of course, he should go Wendy had said.

He did and nothing changed between Wendy and Adam. If anything, they saw more of each other. They would meet up somewhere random and walk and talk.

Their relationship was so deep.

Adam told her he needed her; not just physically; that was a no brainer; they trusted each other implicitly and she had done things with Adam that she wouldn't have dreamt of doing with anyone else.

Wendy believed him. Even when he told her that

him and Kate were going to marry; she knew him even saying it to her was bittersweet.

It was time for Wendy to slow down the joy ride and get out.

It truly broke her heart. She felt bereft without him; her phone not continuously buzzing with messages would look at her as if mocking; she started to get into the habit of burying it in the bottom of her bag.

As soon as restrictions lifted Wendy virtually moved into the golf course; but even there she had reminders of Adam.

During lockdown he had decorated the 19th hole; they'd had sex in the toilets, drank coffee and had sex on the chairs and ate fish and chips sitting on the bar not long after they'd had sex on it.

Even the wallpaper in her living room seemed to mock her.

Wendy had wholeheartedly supported Adam marrying Kate; but by doing that she had sacrificed some of herself. She was a daft old fool.

Some of the golf girls were booking a weekend away in the sun to play golf; restrictions had lifted enough for that to happen. Wendy booked on and took to channelling all her energy into her golf and less on Adam Mitchell.

It was just what the doctor ordered.

The golf, the sun, the banter off her friends and some flirting with a few men playing golf made her put all thoughts of young Adam Mitchell to the back of her mind.

Until he text her.

With Wendy no longer being a slave to her mobile phone she hadn't even bothered switching it on when she had arrived in Spain. The kids knew where she was if they needed her; beyond that who would be texting her.

So it wasn't until they landed back in Newcastle did she even switch it on. And there it was. Despite the fact that he was a married man and there had been months and months of no contact; he wanted to go around and see her.

Wendy's heart lurched.

The sensible thing was to message him back, tell him no and block him.

What she actually did was apologise for not answering sooner; and told him yes.

And the rest like they say is history.

Wendy Carr and Adam Mitchell. The odd couple. Best friends. Lovers. Adulterers.

Despite all of that; whatever it was that they had ran deep.

They saw each other when they could. Sometimes it would be weeks; they would message and sometimes that was enough. Other times the physical pull was too much and they would snatch time where they could; sometimes for weeks on end and then it would cool down again.

Wendy couldn't think about Kate finding out. There was no relationship to be had with Adam. But while she had Adam there was no relationship for her to have with anyone else; he made her feel alive like no one other; just with a message.

It was a situation that Wendy refused to overthink.

All Wendy could do was accept the situation; live her life in between and continue to fizz like only she knew how.

Que Sera Sera!

'Someone who just gets you, everything is easier when you are together. Life is harmonious, laughter is plenty and conversation flows. The only person in the world who understands you completely. The one you can't live without!'

My Person

Epilogue

And that is it.

£10 note HE75 229564 has long been back in circulation; who knows; any one of you may have had it in your possession.

And now it is time to let go of my 'Noters' too.

I think I will always remain friends with a lot of them; we have a Watsapp group; and even though I will watch with interest how each and every one of their lives develop; there will be no more Note books.

From beginning to end it has expanded over 10 years; we have got to know the characters well; we have seen all types of humanity first hand. It's been reality TV through a book.

I cannot thank the people who I have written about enough. There was not one of them that said 'you can't write about that!' Even though for one or two of them; they may have lives that blow up when the Last Note is published.

All I can do is wish each and every one of them good luck; I won't say goodbye; just cheerio for now.

As for me, I've got some new publications coming out. A couple of them even got a mention in this book:

LAST NOTE

Cushie Butterfield
Who Said That?
Mack Book

Keep an eye out for them.

Thank you to everyone who has bought my Note Books, your encouragement and support.

Love, Gill

'Don't Cry Because it's Over – Smile Because it Happened!'

Dr Seuss

Printed in Great Britain
by Amazon